"DO YOU KNOW, MISS TERRINGTON, WHAT I THOUGHT THE VERY FIRST TIME I CLAPPED EYES ON YOU?"

She looked curious, and then a warm glow of color infused her face as she apparently recalled that the first place he had seen her was in his bedchamber. "I am sure I do not," she said, her eyes fixed at a point somewhere over his shoulder.

"What I thought, Miss Terrington," he continued, "was that you looked like an elf. What the crofters call a *sithiche,* a mischievous sprite come from the glens to lead me back along the Low Road to the Highlands. Then you opened your lips to bark orders and questions at me, and I was certain you were a *tannasg* instead, come to pester me into perdition. In the days since, I've come to think I was right."

Her cheeks flushed brighter with indignation. "I'm not so bad as that!"

"Aye, lass." He grinned, carrying her hand up to his lips for another kiss. "You are. But do not worry yourself over it. I am a soldier, and used to fighting for what I want. Now come, I am sure your aunt must be wondering where you've gone."

BOOK YOUR PLACE ON OUR WEBSITE AND MAKE THE READING CONNECTION!

We've created a customized website just for our very special readers, where you can get the inside scoop on everything that's going on with Zebra, Pinnacle and Kensington books.

When you come online, you'll have the exciting opportunity to:

- View covers of upcoming books
- Read sample chapters
- Learn about our future publishing schedule (listed by publication month *and author*)
- Find out when your favorite authors will be visiting a city near you
- Search for and order backlist books from our online catalog
- Check out author bios and background information
- Send e-mail to your favorite authors
- Meet the Kensington staff online
- Join us in weekly chats with authors, readers and other guests
- Get writing guidelines
- AND MUCH MORE!

**Visit our website at
http://www.zebrabooks.com**

THE
SCOTSMAN
AND THE
SPINSTER

Carolyn Madison

Zebra Books
Kensington Publishing Corp.
http://www.zebrabooks.com

ZEBRA BOOKS are published by

Kensington Publishing Corp.
850 Third Avenue
New York, NY 10022

First Printing: July, 2000
10 9 8 7 6 5 4 3 2 1

Printed in the United States of America

This book is dedicated to the memory of Robert Bush.
With love, from Anthony and Tyler Iszler

Prologue

Spain, 1813
Alvares

"Get down, blast your bloody hides!" Sergeant Ross MacCailan roared the command over the staccato burst of gunfire. The ambush had come out of nowhere, taking him and the rest of the patrol by surprise. Two soldiers were dead and two more were wounded before he succeeded in guiding them to the dubious safety of the abandoned stone cottage. Now they were pinned down by heavy fire, and the devil of it was he had no idea who was shooting at them. Given the uncertain conditions in Spain, it could be French Regulars, Spanish partisans, or even British deserters willing to slaughter their own comrades for whatever poor trinkets they possessed.

"Corporal Roberts to me!" he shouted, firing at the stand of trees where the murderous shot continued unabated.

A huge man, his face blackened by gunpowder, crawled over to join him at the window. "Aye, Sergeant?"

"How many are there, do you think?" Ross demanded, his sharp green gaze never leaving the trees as he reloaded his rifle.

The corporal fired his own rifle before answering. "Could be ten, I'd say, perhaps more. Not *guerrillas,* though, else we'd all be dead. French, I'm thinking, or maybe not," he added, ducking as a musket ball screamed through the air just above his head. "Them Frogs don't shoot half so well."

Despite the gravity of the situation, a wry grin split Ross's lean face. It quickly faded as he turned his mind to more prosaic matters. "How many men have we injured?"

"Three. The lieutenant's the worst; gut-shot."

Ross tore his gaze away from the window long enough to glance toward the corner of the room where a young man lay softly moaning. The front of his uniform tunic was already stained black with blood, and his face was ashen with the rapid approach of death. Much as Ross's heart ached, he accepted there was nothing he could do and turned back to the window.

"Take his rifle and spread his ammunition amongst the others," he ordered. "Tell them to start firing at thirty-second intervals, and to stop once they've gone through half their ammunition."

A look of crafty understanding stole into the older man's eyes. "Aye, lad. Have a plan, do ye?"

Ross thrust back a strand of sweat-dampened blond hair that had fallen across his forehead and nodded. "Perhaps. Have them ready to fire on my order."

Over the next twenty minutes the soldiers in the small cottage bravely held off their attackers, the rain of fire they loosed punishing the unseen enemy. But soon the shooting grew sporadic: eight shots, then five, then two, then none. An unearthly silence descended upon the clearing as Ross and his men waited for whatever came next.

"Come on, you sorry sots, come on," he whispered softly, his rifle clenched in his hands. "We've no ammunition left, we're sitting here waiting for you to slaughter us. Come on."

As if in response to his muttered imprecations, a voice called out in accented English. "You in the cottage, surrender in the name of the emperor!"

"French," the corporal grumbled, crawling over to join Ross at the window. "May the devil take the lot of them!"

"He will," Ross replied, then cautiously raised his head. "What guarantee have I you will not harm my men?" he called out, affecting the elegant tones of a gentleman.

"Why, my word as one officer to another," came the mocking reply. "Surrender, *monsieur.* My patience grows thin."

"Now what?" the corporal asked. "The bloody fool thinks you're an officer."

As this was Ross's intention, he wasn't concerned. Instead, he glanced back at the corner where the lieutenant lay sprawled in the stillness of death. The lad had done them little good in life, he reflected. Mayhap in death he would serve a better use.

"Move all but two men to this side," he told Roberts. "When the French show themselves, be ready to fire at my signal."

The corporal gave a slow nod of understanding. "Aye, lad, I ken. But do ye know what ye're about? Ye'll be placing yerself between our fire and theirs. Ye're like to get blown to hell."

Ross didn't respond. After fifteen years in the Army he'd faced death too many times to give the matter of his mortality any thought. If he died, he died, but in the meanwhile it was his intention to take as many French with him as he could manage.

"I would negotiate with you for the safety of my men," he called out again, this time in impeccable French. "Step into the open that I might see you and know you mean what you say."

"You are scarce in a position to make demands, *mon ami*," the French officer replied, clearly amused. "But I will do as you wish. Be so kind as to come outside. Hands up, if you please."

"I am wounded and cannot stand," Ross replied, accepting the pistols from Corporal Roberts and tucking them into the waistband of his leather breeches. "My sergeant will be with me."

There was another silence. "Very well, but no tricks, I warn you. One wrong move, and you are a dead man, *comprehend?*"

"Mais oui," Ross answered, and crossed the room to gaze down at the lieutenant. In death the pompous officer who had been the bane of Ross's existence looked pathetically young. How old had he been? Ross mused. Twenty? He doubted the lad had even bedded his first woman, and wondered if whoever had purchased the youth his commission had any idea they'd sent him to his death.

Pushing back his bleak thoughts, Ross bent and hefted the lieutenant to his feet. "Sorry, Lieutenant Mackelby," he said, turning toward the door. "But you're about to become a hero."

The rough clearing in front of the cottage was filled with French soldiers, all of whom trained their weapons on Ross as he stepped out into the watery sunlight. There were ten, he noted, including the two officers mounted on high-stepping grays. Ross concentrated on the captain, and in the other man's cold eyes he could see his intention to kill him and the others the moment they surrendered.

He stepped forward cautiously, keeping the lieutenant's body slightly in front of him to hide the fact he was armed. "My lieutenant has fainted," he said, exaggerating the Scottish accent he'd all but lost a decade earlier. "I do no' think I can hold him much longer."

"Then drop him, Sergeant, and order the others to come out," the captain said mockingly, drawing a pistol and aiming it at Ross's head. "I grow weary of this game."

"Yes, sir," Ross said, bending his legs and carefully lowering the lieutenant to the ground. When he was confident he had everyone's full attention, he shoved the body to one side and dove for cover.

"Fire!" he yelled, rolling to the side and firing. His bullet struck the captain in the center of his forehead, and even as the courtyard exploded with gunfire, Ross had the satisfaction of seeing the officer tumble dead from his horse.

The battle was short but decisive and when the shooting stopped, all of the French soldiers lay dead. Ross felt neither satisfaction nor elation, merely a grim numbness that blocked out everything else. He confiscated the dead officers' horses to help transport the wounded, and then he and the others dug graves for the dead. Before leaving, he pocketed Lieutenant Mackelby's personal effects, knowing his family would want them.

Several hours later he and the remaining men limped their way into the encampment. Ross was filthy, hungry as a wolf, and exhausted beyond the point of collapse. He knew he should report to the captain, but he was too exhausted to care. There would be time enough later to give an accounting, he told himself wearily, and in the end it would make little difference. The dead would be no less dead for the wait.

He ducked into the ragged excuse of a tent he shared with three other men, and had only just begun undressing when a young major lifted the flap and came scurrying inside.

"Hurry, man, hurry! We've no time to wait!" he exclaimed, so wild-eyed Ross thought the camp was under attack.

"What is it? The French?" he asked, reaching automatically for the rifle that was never out of reach.

"No, it is the general!" the other man cried, dancing from one foot to another in his agitation. "He is in the camp and asking for you!"

Ross relaxed at learning it was no more than that. General Callingham was a terror to his junior officers to be sure, but Ross had served with him long enough to know he wouldn't fault him for taking a few minutes to eat.

"I thank you for telling me, Major," he said, forcing himself to respond courteously when what he really wanted to do was throw the fellow out on his ear. "Pray present General Callingham with my compliments, and tell him I shall report as soon as I—"

"No, not the general," the major interrupted. *"The general!* 'Tis Wellington himself! Hurry, we cannot keep him waiting!"

Had the man been any less excited, Ross would have suspected him of playing a trick on him. He was still suspicious, but accepted there was little he could do: an order was an order. He reached for the jacket he'd just discarded.

"You can't mean to go wearing that!" the Major gasped, pointing a trembling finger at the front of Ross's uniform.

Ross glanced down at the blood staining the jacket and shrugged. " 'Tis French blood."

"But—"

"Major," Ross interrupted, scowling, "you can have me fast, or you can have me clean. You canno' have both."

In the end the young officer decided a clean sergeant would make a better impression than a dirty one, and he granted Ross a scant half hour to make himself presentable. Thirty minutes later Ross found himself being presented to the great general, while half the command staff looked on in interest and obvious resentment. General Arthur Wellesley, only recently elevated to the rank of Earl of Wellington, was geniality itself as he thanked the officers and then dismissed them in a manner that was polite, but unmistakable. The moment they were alone, he turned back to Ross with a decided twinkle in his eyes.

" 'Tis a wonder we manage to win a single battle, with dolts like that leading the way," he observed, shaking his head. "Ah, well, at least they usually have the good grace to get themselves killed before causing too much harm."

Ross thought of the young lieutenant he had buried a few hours earlier, and held his tongue. "Is there something I can do for you, my lord?" he asked, remaining rigidly at attention.

If Wellington sensed his resentment he ignored it, giving him an enigmatic smile instead. "Eventually, Sergeant, eventually. In the meanwhile, you must allow me to congratulate you on your accession to the peerage . . . Viscount St. Jerome."

Ross jerked his head back in shock. "My uncle is dead?"

"These three months past," the general said, handing Ross a franked letter. "The mails are a trifle slow, I fear."

Ross accepted the letter numbly, noting the waxed seal had already been broken. The loss of privacy this indicated should have enraged him, but he felt only a vague indifference. "There has been some mistake, sir," he said, not bothering to open the letter. "My uncle must surely have disinherited me years ago in favor of my cousin. 'Tis him you should be congratulating, not me. I am no English lord." He made to hand the letter back.

"Ah, but you are, sir, you are," Wellesley said, folding his arms across his chest and ignoring Ross's gesture. "Whatever his feelings toward you, your uncle had no legal grounds to break the entailment. You are the only son of his only brother, and as such, you are rightfully next in line for the title. Your cousin, I believe, is descended from the female line. Rail against it however you will, Sergeant, you cannot change that fact. You *are* the viscount."

Ross clenched his hands, a black rage descending upon him at the memory of the rigid, mean-spirited man who had been his uncle. Douglas MacCailan had long since forgotten his clan name and honor, and he'd never forgiven Ross's father for returning to the Highlands in defiance of his wishes. When his father died, his uncle had ordered Ross brought to London, dangling the promise of a commission if Ross did as he was told. Ross's response had been to join the Army as a common soldier, and he'd thought that the end of the matter. It seemed, however, he'd neglected to consider the vagaries of English law.

"To the devil with him and with his bloody title!" he cried, not caring if his insolence won him a thousand lashes. "I am a soldier, a Scot, not some prancing fool of an Englishman!" Then he broke off, appalled at what he had said and to whom he had said it.

To his surprise, the general actually chuckled. "And I am an Irishman who more than shares your opinion of the majority of English gentlemen, Sergeant MacCailan. A more sorry and useless lot I've yet to see, but that's neither here nor there. Agents of your uncle will be arriving in camp tomorrow, and when they do, you, sir, shall be leaving with them."

Ross rubbed his head, abruptly weary of this ridiculous conversation. "General, I mean no offense, but I—"

"Sergeant," Wellington interrupted, his voice gentle, "you said you are a soldier, and so you are, a damned fine one, from all accounts. And as a soldier you must know there are times when sacrifices must be made; when the wants of one man must be set aside for the greater good of the regiment. Is that not so?"

"Aye," Ross agreed reluctantly, wondering what the general was prattling on about. "I know."

"You've fought well, lad, and I am grateful to you for all you have done. Now I am asking you to help me fight a different sort of battle, a battle I greatly fear we are about to lose."

Ross stirred uneasily. Despite the disdain he felt for the pampered officers he'd been forced to serve under, he'd become friends with one or two of them, and through them he had learned much of London gossip. "You are speaking of the debates," he said, understanding at last the reason for the general's visit.

The older man nodded. "I am. We fight day to day to drive Napoleon from this godforsaken place, paying in good English blood for every cursed inch of ground we gain. But even as we have victory within our grasp, those pompous fools in London risk throwing all of it away. If these newest acts pass I will be recalled, and our Army will be put under the command of some useless Society pet more acceptable to those blue-blooded idiots. Well, I will not let that happen to me or to my men, do you hear me, sir? I will not!"

Ross fell into a brooding silence as he considered Wellington's words. "I understand you want me to accept the title that I might cast my vote for you in the House of Lords," he said. "And so I should, if I thought it would do a whit of good. But I do not see that it will. I am but one man. How can I make any difference?"

The general's response was a wolfish smile. "One man, Sergeant, can make all the difference in the world, provided he is the *right* man."

Ross blinked up at him in confusion. "But I am a sergeant, and a Scotsman in the bargain; no fine title or fortune will ever change that. Those blue bloods you speak of won't so much as glance in my direction."

Wellington raised an imperious eyebrow. "Have you ever known me not to have a plan or two tucked up my sleeve?" Before Ross could respond, he handed him a second letter.

"Take this, and go to the address I've written down. When you get there, whatever the person there tells you to do, you are to do it. No questions, no arguments. Just carry out their orders as you would my own. Is that clear?"

Ross accepted the letter reluctantly. "General—"

"Sergeant, I do not ask this lightly," Wellington said, his expression grave as he met Ross's gaze. "Your commanding officers all speak highly of your bravery and your loyalty, qualities I shall stand in sore need of in the coming months. If I had a choice I should keep you here at my side, but I do not have that choice. And neither, sir, do you. If you wish to help me and the men under my command, you must accept the title and return to England. There is no other way."

Ross gazed down at the address scribbled across the letter.

A. Terrington, Number Eleven Bruton Street. Who was that? he wondered. Some political crony of the general's, he didn't doubt. A doddering old man who would take him under his wing and teach him how to go about. Ross wished he could toss both letters into the flames and walk away, but he knew he could not. The wily old soldier was right, he thought bitterly. There was no other way.

"Sergeant?" Wellington was watching him intently. "What say you? Will you carry out my orders, or will you not?"

Ross gave the letters a final glare before drawing himself to attention. "Yes, General," he said, mentally consigning the older man to perdition even as he snapped off a sharp salute. "I will carry out your orders."

One

"No, no, no, my lord," Miss Adalaide Terrington exclaimed, prying her pupil's fingers from about the delicate china cup. " 'Tis a cup of tea you are holding, not a mug of ale! Relax your grip, else you will shatter the cup."

"Y-yes, Miss Terrington," the terrified young man stammered, the tortuous knot of his cravat bobbing up and down as he swallowed. "As—as you say, Miss Terrington."

"Very good," Addy said soothingly, fighting the urge to box his ears. She and the newest Earl of Hixworth had been hard at work all morning, and her patience, never strong under the best of circumstances, was wearing dangerously thin. Gritting her teeth, she drew a deep breath and began anew.

"Now," she said, sitting back in her chair and fixing him with her sternest look, "let us pretend you are taking tea with a lady, Lady Devington, let us say, and—"

"Lady Devington?" the dandy squeaked, his pale eyes

widening in horror. Too late Addy recalled his puppy crush on the haughty beauty, and before she could recant he clenched his fingers, shattering the tiny teacup and sending bits of china and drops of tepid tea flying.

Addy watched the unfolding catastrophe with glum resignation, mentally congratulating herself for her foresight in not serving the tea at its proper temperature. Scalded pupils seldom gave good references.

"It's all right," she said, reaching for the bell pull. "No, don't cry," she added when his chin began wobbling precariously. "How many times must I tell you, *gentlemen* do not cry."

"I am sorry, Miss Terrington," he said, blinking back his tears and struggling manfully not to disgrace himself. "I shall endeavor to do better. You—you won't tell anyone, will you?" He cast her a look of earnest appeal.

Behind the lenses of her spectacles, Addy raised her blue eyes heavenward in a mute plea for forbearance. "Of course not, my lord," she said, assuming her most haughty demeanor. "I am your instructress, and as such, I am sworn to secrecy."

"You are too kind, ma'am," he responded, dabbing at his forehead with his handkerchief. "But the simple truth is I'm no good at this Society taradiddle, no good at all. The very thought of being in the same room as a lady makes me quake with fear, upon my soul, it does."

As this was a confidence she had heard many times in the past, Addy had a soothing reply at the ready. "We all have our fears, Lord Hixworth," she said calmly, "but it falls to us to conquer them. And for your information, I am quite certain many of those young ladies you go in such terror of are every bit as afraid of you as you are of them. After all, *you* are an earl, and heir to one of the most respectable titles in England."

He looked much struck by that. "I am, aren't I?"

"Indeed," she assured him, ladling on the sauce with a liberal, if not altogether honest, hand. "And you are by far one of the most graceful dancers it has ever been my privilege to partner. You have mastered the quadrille, have you not?"

The earl rubbed his nose and looked thoughtful. "Monsieur Rochelles did say I have a pretty leg," he allowed, a cautious note of optimism creeping into his voice.

"And I heard Mr. Lauretens remark that you sit a horse like an Ajax," Addy agreed, happy to be telling the truth about something, at least. "So you see, sir, you have much to recommend you as *un parti par excellence*. There isn't the slightest reason for you to fear a mere tea party, is there?"

"No," he said, giving a decisive nod. "No, by Jove, there's not. Thank you, Miss Terrington." And he beamed at her like a proud schoolboy.

An hour later the now delighted earl took his leave, showing off his newfound confidence by kissing Addy's hand. The door had scarce closed behind him before Addy's aunt, Lady Matilda Fareham, who always acted as chaperon during the instruction sessions, glanced up from her knitting.

"Really, child, I do not see how you can abide feeding that dolt's vanity as you do," she chided, a look of disapproval stamped on her lined features. "Have you no shame?"

"Very little, as a matter of fact," Addy replied, unfazed by her aunt's scolding. "And there's no harm in flattering another person when it's all to the good. However rough his manners, Lord Hixworth is possessed of a generous heart. I shall have to make certain to find him an heiress who will appreciate it."

"It is your own heart you should be looking after, if you want my opinion," Lady Fareham said, shaking her knitting at Addy. "You are scarce out of your girlhood, and a beauty as well. You ought to be keeping a string of beaus dangling after you, instead of bear-leading a bunch of cubs through Season after Season."

Addy hid a grin at the overly generous description of herself. "And you dare have the cheek to accuse me of employing false flattery," she said, chuckling as she poured herself a cup of tea. "Come, ma'am, we both know I am five and twenty, possessed of features no more than passingly fair, and am accursed with hair as red as it is unruly."

"Furthermore," she added, before her aunt could sputter a protest, "I am also a sharp-tongued bluestocking, a termagant of the first water, and I am, or so I have heard Reginald claim too many times to number, completely ineligible as a bride."

Lady Fareham thrust out her bottom lip in a pout. "You needn't sound so pleased with yourself," she grumbled.

"Oh, but I am pleased," Addy said, her eyes dancing with satisfaction. "A chit still considered on the Marriage Mart should never experience half the freedom as I do. Nor would she be permitted to instruct gentlemen in the refined arts, however ably chaperoned. Why, before I put on my caps and began spouting Latin at anyone who would listen, there was even unpleasant gossip when I showed Cousin Teddy how to go about. *Cousin Teddy,* of all people!" She shook her head at the vicious rumor that had had all the cats dining on her reputation two Seasons earlier.

"Perhaps," Lady Fareham conceded truculently, "but I still—"

The sound of a terrible commotion from the front hall drowned out the rest of her observation, and even as Addy was leaping to her feet to investigate, a voice called out excitedly.

"Miss Terrington! Miss Terrington! Come quickly!"

Not knowing what she would find, Addy snatched up the poker from the fireplace and dashed out into the hall to protect the household from whatever was menacing them. She found her staff crowded into the entryway, huddled around a figure lying sprawled on the stoop.

"Who is it?" she asked, crowding closer for a better look.

"I don't know, miss," Williams, the butler, said, kneeling beside the prone man. "A sergeant in the Rifles, I should say, judging from his uniform."

Addy gently elbowed the housekeeper aside and knelt on the other side of the unconscious man. "Is he drunk?" she asked, taking in his travel-stained and somewhat threadbare appearance with a worried gaze.

"I don't know, miss, but I do not believe so," Williams replied, gently turning the man onto his back. "There's no smell of the drink to him, and truth to tell, he doesn't look the sort to get jug-bit."

Addy shot him an incredulous look, wondering if her major-domo had taken temporary leave of his senses.

The unconscious man on the ground was as rough and crude as any she had ever seen, and to her gaze he gave every appearance of being precisely the sort to lose himself in a bottle . . . after first losing himself in the arms of the nearest available doxy. Then she looked at his face, and in his harsh and utterly masculine countenance, she could see the truth of Williams's observation.

He was handsome enough, she mused objectively, and his high cheekbones, aquiline nose, and finely shaped blond brows gave mute testimony to an ancestry that was far more aristocratic than his humble rank would seem to indicate. But it was his stern mouth and strong jaw that caught and held her attention, for these were to her the true indication of his character. Both bespoke a strong will and indomitable spirit, and she found it difficult to believe that a man possessing those traits would drink himself into a stupor. No, there had to be more to it than that, she decided, laying her hand on his lean cheek.

"Good heavens!" she exclaimed, snatching her fingers back at once. "The poor man is burning with fever!"

Williams scrambled back from the man in horror. "He is *diseased?* " he gasped, a look of revulsion twisting his usually impassive features.

Her concentration now fully centered on the sergeant, Addy did no more than send him a disapproving scowl. "He is ill, Williams; there is a difference." She glanced up and caught the eye of one of the footmen. "Go at once for Dr. Trevey," she ordered, "and ask him to come as quickly as he is able. The others of you help carry the sergeant into the house."

"Adalaide, you can not mean to bring this—this person into our home," Lady Fareham protested, even as the young footman dashed off to carry out Addy's instructions. "Why, we know nothing of him, not even his name! He could be anyone!"

"Precisely, Aunt," Addy replied, her mind firmly set. "He could be anyone, including one of my beloved brothers. Were one of them to be in such a state, I should hope whoever found them would do all in their power to render them every assistance."

"Well, at least try to learn something of him," her aunt returned, impatiently acknowledging Addy's point. "He could have family nearby, and was trying to reach them when he collapsed."

Since this seemed only logical, Addy began cautiously patting the sergeant's pockets. Inside his uniform jacket she found a letter and drew it out, her eyebrows rising when she saw it was addressed to her. Her eyebrows rose even higher when she turned the letter over and saw the seal pressed into the red wax. *Good heavens!* she thought in astonishment. Why on earth would Lord Wellington be writing her? She broke the wax seal and unfolded the letter. When she was finished reading, she carefully refolded it and rose to her feet.

"Please put his lordship in my father's old room," she said coolly. "I will be upstairs in a few moments."

"His lordship?" Lady Fareham repeated, stepping aside as the footmen hurried forward. "You mean you have learned who he is?"

"Yes, I have," Addy answered, keeping an eagle eye on the footmen as they struggled into the house with their burden.

"Well?" her aunt demanded when Addy refused to elaborate. "Who is he, then?"

"He is Viscount St. Jerome. I am to turn him into a gentleman," Addy said, and then scurried after the footmen, ignoring her aunt's cries for further intelligence.

Images exploded in Ross's mind, bright and deadly as the flash of cannon fire in battle. He could see his mother's face as she bent down to kiss him, her green eyes, which she had bequeathed him, soft with love and affection. He saw his father's face as he'd last seen it, wasted and thin with illness as he lay dying. Even his uncle's face swam before him, pinched and full of haughty pride as he ordered Ross to join him in London.

There were other faces as well. The faces of the men he had served with, men he had seen die horrifying deaths, and men he had been forced to kill as he'd fought desperately for his life. These last images troubled him most, and he moved his head restlessly as he sought to escape them.

"It's all right," he heard a voice say as a cool cloth was laid on his forehead. "You're in England now. It's all right."

England? Ross frowned fretfully and decided the voice was mistaken. He was in Spain, preparing for the siege at Badajoz. The general had given him orders to . . . to . . . His brows knit in thought as he struggled to capture the elusive memory.

"The fever seems to be breaking," the voice said, sounding pleased. "Perhaps that pest of a doctor knew what he was about after all. I should never have credited it."

"Please, miss, do go along now," another voice spoke anxiously. "It ain't proper, your being here. Her ladyship will screech like a cat do she hear of it."

"Then we shall have to make certain she never hears of it, won't we?" the first voice returned, and Ross grinned at the sharpness of vinegar in her tone. Clearly the lady was a force to be reckoned with, and Ross wondered what she looked like. Perhaps when these accursed wars were ended, he would return to England and see if he could find her. It had been many years since he'd last flirted with a lady . . .

When he next regained consciousness Ross was able to open his eyes, and what he saw had him blinking in astonishment. The room he was in was nearly as fine as the rooms he'd glimpsed at his uncle's house. The walls were covered in rich, green damask, and the furnishings he could see were constructed of delicately crafted mahogany that gleamed in the light of the dancing fire. Ross stared at the flames in confusion, trying to remember how he might have come to such a place.

His last clear memory was being in a filthy dockside *taverna,* waiting for transportation to England. General Wellesley had arranged a cabin on the first available ship for him and the two officious fools who'd come to collect him.

"The general!" Ross bolted up in bed, only to collapse with a moan as the room did a sickening whirl about him.

"There are no generals here, my lord, and that will teach you not to make any more foolish moves."

The voice Ross remembered from the first time he'd awakened sounded to his right, and he cautiously turned his head to find a young woman sitting beside his bed.

His first thought was that she looked like an elf. She was tiny, an inch or so above five feet, with delicate features and a mass of curly red hair stuffed beneath a starched muslin cap. A pair of gold-rimmed spectacles were perched on her snub nose, and behind the lenses a pair of bright blue eyes regarded him with frank speculation. Ross stared at her for several seconds before blurting out the first words to cross his mind.

"Who the devil are you?"

"I am Miss Adalaide Terrington," she replied, her soft voice surprisingly firm. "The Earl of Wellington has instructed me to prepare you for Society."

Years of hiding every emotion were all that kept Ross from gaping at her like a slack-jawed idiot. Perhaps the illness he was suffering had affected his reasoning, he thought, studying the young woman warily. Wellington had made no mention of an instructor, and he certainly hadn't said anything about that instructor being a female. Then he remembered the final order the general had given him, and his eyes narrowed in suspicion.

"You're A. Terrington?" he demanded coldly.

"Yes, Adalaide Terrington, as I have already explained," she replied, frowning at him in obvious displeasure. "Are you feeling quite the thing, my lord? Dr. Trevey assured me that the fever shouldn't affect your mental faculties, but one never knows. Perhaps I should send for him and—"

"There's no need to fetch a doctor, Miss Terrington, I am fine," Ross interrupted, shoving his hair off his forehead with a shaking hand. In truth, he felt like bloody hell, but he wasn't so lost to the proprieties as to admit such a thing to a lady; even a lady as appallingly blunt as this one appeared to be. He was also loath to admit he was in anything other than fighting trim. Something told him this one would be quick to take advantage of any weakness.

"That is good," she returned with an approving nod. "For we've much to accomplish, and precious little time in which to accomplish it. We'll begin by ascertaining your current level of knowledge. What is the correct way to address a duke?"

"The devil!" Ross exclaimed, wondering if perhaps *she* was the one whose mental faculties weren't all that they should be.

"No, it's 'your grace,' actually," she returned calmly. "A duke might well indeed be a devil, especially a few of the royal ones, but one must never address a duke as such. An earl is properly styled as 'my lord,' as is a marquess, and a viscount. A baronet is never addressed as 'my lord,' but is rather called—"

"I don't give a tinker's damn what he's called!" Ross interrupted, more certain than ever that he was in the presence of a Bedlamite. "I'm not learning this rot!"

"Of course you are. How else do you expect to get on once you take your seat in the House of Lords?"

The calm question and the superior look accompanying it had Ross cursing Wellington anew. On the journey from London the talk was all of the debate before Parliament, and what would happen if Old Nosey, as most of the troops called the general, was to be recalled. Even half dead from the fever raging through him, Ross had attended their words, and the fear and unease he'd heard had made him that much more determined to do all in his power to prevent that from happening. The pox take the general and Miss Terrington, he thought sourly. He was well and truly trapped.

"That is better," she said. It was plain by the smug look on his inquisitor's face that she correctly took his sullen silence for acquiescence. "Now, as I was saying, a baronet is not a lord, but rather is referred to as 'Sir.' Is that clear, or shall I write it down for you?"

" 'Tis clear, and 'tis something I already knew," Ross replied with a disgruntled scowl. "The first thing a common soldier learns is what to call his betters. One mistake, and he could find himself lashed to the whipping post."

That seemed to take her aback. "I see," she said after a few moments. "Well, you needn't fear I shall be quite that severe, my lord. Do you know as well the proper ranking for titles?"

"Aye," Ross said, and proved it by rattling them off for her. His answers must have met with her approval, because she quickly moved on to the next topic.

"Your solicitor came by while you were sleeping, and he was most upset. It seems you gave him and his associate the slip at the docks, and they feared you'd met with some unpleasantness. Taking into account the fact you were suffering the effects of the fever, I must take leave to tell you that such things are simply not done. You're a viscount now, and you've obligations to the title and to those under your protection."

She continued prattling on, setting down an eye-popping list of what she called his duties. Ross listened in mounting resentment, his temper held tightly in check. When she paused for breath, he spoke for the first time.

"I am a soldier, Miss Terrington. No one understands better what duty and honor mean. Do not presume to lecture me about such things again."

Instead of demurring, she had the audacity to bristle with indignation. "I beg your pardon. It wasn't my intention to offend."

Ross leaned forward, wrapping his fingers about her arm before she had the chance to pull away. " 'Tis little matter what you intended," he retorted, his narrowed gaze capturing hers, "for offend me you have. I am more than aware of all that rests on my actions, and you've no' the right to question my determination to do it. Is that clear, Miss Terrington, or must I write it down for *you?* "

Her mouth opened as if to disagree, and then she clearly thought better of it. "That won't be necessary, Lord St. Jerome," she responded in accents as stiff as her posture. "I understand perfectly."

He held her arm a second longer, and then released her. "Then mind you remember it," he said, abruptly weary. He lay back on the pillows, closing his eyes and tumbling headlong into the blackness of sleep.

The next three days passed in a haze of fever and exhaustion. Ross spent most of the time sleeping, but when he awoke it was usually to find the redoubtable Miss Terrington at his bedside. There were often lessons of some sort, and at her insistence he gave her leave to engage the services of a valet for him. The valet, a rather diffident young man named Joseph, saw to his more personal needs, something Ross found singularly embarrassing. He had been on his own too long to tolerate such cosseting, and he resented being tended like a helpless babe.

Four days after arriving in London, Ross left his room for the first time. He was still shakier than he cared admitting, but he was done with convalescing. As Miss Terrington had pointed out, time was a commodity of which they had precious little, and he wasn't about to waste another second of it lying about like a pasha in a harem.

Thanks to his uncle's solicitors his trunks had arrived shortly after he had, but Joseph pronounced most of the contents "unacceptable for a gentleman." In the end Ross donned his best uniform before going downstairs in search of his hostess. It wasn't difficult finding her. He simply followed the sound of raised voices to a parlor located in the front of the house.

"A scandal, that's what it is, a scandal!" he heard a shrill female voice exclaim. "Allowing a gentleman to remain under your roof when you are unmarried! Whatever shall people say?"

"Considering Arthur and Aunt Matilda were both here to act as chaperons, very little, I should think," came Miss Terrington's sharp response. "And for your information, Beatrice, the poor man was half dead from the fever! Even had he wanted to ravish me, he wouldn't have possessed the strength to do it."

Ross raised his eyebrows at that. Evidently the impression he'd made on the little *bencheard* was poorer than he'd thought, else she wouldn't be harboring any doubts about his masculine abilities. Having learned the value of timing from Wellington, Ross judged this the perfect moment in which to make his appearance. Straightening the collar of his uniform, he pushed open the door and strode boldly into the room.

The three people in the room turned to look at him, and the look of embarrassed horror stamped on their faces had him fighting back a satisfied grin. It came as no surprise that Miss Terrington was the first to recover her *sang-froid*, her manner smoothly polished as she rose to greet him.

"Lord St. Jerome," she said, offering him a cool smile along with her slender hand. "I didn't know you had left your room. You are quite recovered, I trust?" She was dressed in a delicate gown of soft green silk with a ribbon of darker green velvet laced beneath her breasts, and her resemblance to a woodland fairy was even more pronounced.

"Quite recovered, Miss Terrington," he drawled, his eyes meeting hers as he carried her hand to his lips. "In all respects." He added this last with a wolfish smile of delight.

A delicate blush was the only sign that she comprehended his meaning, and he had to give the minx her due as she turned to introduce him to the room's other occupants.

"My lord, I should like to make you known to my brother, Mr. Reginald Terrington, and his wife, Beatrice. Beatrice, Reggie, allow me to present His Lordship, Viscount St. Jerome."

"My lord." Reginald Terrington rose belatedly to his feet, dragging his plump wife up with him. " 'Tis an honor to meet you."

"Mrs. Terrington, Mr. Terrington." Ross inclined his

head in deliberate condescension. Having been on the receiving end of such patronizing behavior too many years to count, he rather enjoyed acting the haughty aristocrat.

"Lord St. Jerome, how delightful to meet you," Mrs. Terrington purred, pushing herself past Miss Terrington to bat her lashes at him. "You must allow me to invite you to reside in our home during your convalescence. We live on Upper Brook Street, and I am certain you will find the surroundings *far* more agreeable to a gentleman of your rank."

Her fawning manner set Ross's teeth on edge. She was eager enough to ingratiate herself with Lord St. Jerome, but he doubted she'd be so obliging to Sergeant MacCailan. Mayhap 'twas time she learned the two were one and the same.

"My rank, Mrs. Terrington, 'tis that of sergeant," he told her, making no effort to disguise his displeasure. "And I promise you this place is as a palace to me. I am content to remain where I am; for the moment, at least."

"But my lord, I fear it will not suit," Mr. Terrington stammered, his pale hands fluttering in protest. "I realize you are new to the peerage, but you must know you risk my sister's reputation by remaining beneath her roof when the two you are not related. Such things are simply not done in *our* world. London ain't Scotland, don't you see."

The insult implied in his words had Ross's eyes narrowing in fury. Even when he'd been the rawest of recruits his pride had never wavered, and he was cursed if he would allow such a slur on his character and his people pass unchallenged.

"You needn't worry over your sister's reputation, Mr. Terrington," he said coldly. "I've a home of my own on

Berkeley Street, and will be repairing there this very afternoon."

He didn't bother mentioning the home was already occupied by his cousin, William Atherton, who, according to his solicitors, seemed in no hurry to leave. Not only did Ross consider the matter none of the Terringtons' affair, he also didn't care if his cousin left the place willingly or nay. Having helped oust the French from Ciudad Rodrigo, he was fairly certain he could dislodge a parasitic dandy without much effort.

"Ah." Mr. Terrington greeted Ross's blunt statement with a strained smile. "That is very good, my lord, very good indeed," he said, tugging nervously at his starched cravat.

They spent the next hour making desultory conversation before the couple took their leave, quitting the room with what could only be termed unflattering haste. Miss Terrington watched them go, her eyes bright with laughter as she turned to Ross.

"That was neatly done, Lord St. Jerome," she said approvingly, her lips curving in a fetching smile. "It is good to know your air of consequence won't require any work to bring you up to snuff."

Ross cast her a suspicious look, certain she was having a great laugh at his expense. "Meaning what?"

"Meaning, sir, that you are already puffed up and imperious as a prince, and you shan't require but a bit of polishing before taking your rightful place in Society."

Ross digested the observation in silence. "Is that compliment or complaint?" he demanded at last.

"Both," his tormentor replied, then chuckled at his outraged expression. "And you needn't cast daggers at me, my lord, for it is all to the better. We *want* you to be an insufferable prig. How else are you to overwhelm your enemy except by superior force? To win, you see, you must be three times as haughty as the highest-born member of the House of Lords. It is the only way you can hope to gain their respect."

To his annoyance, Ross could see the sense of her words. He'd spent half his lifetime observing the ways of the English, and he knew when it came to matters of society and position, the *ton* were without mercy. Did he show the slightest hint of weakness, they would be upon him like a pack of jackals.

"What must I do?" The question was asked without his usual surliness, as he grudgingly accepted he would need her help.

Dimples flashed in her cheeks as her smile deepened. "Why, something I am sure will fill your Scottish heart with delight, Sergeant. You must act as if you don't give that"—she snapped her delicate fingers—"about what they think of you. Believe me, the less you appear to value them, the more they shall value you."

"Now," she continued, before he could gather his wits, "it is time we began working on your bows. A courtly bow you do well enough, but I fear your sardonic bow could do with a spot of polishing. You have been confronted by a gentleman whose cravat is tied in the most appalling fashion, and he dares to force an introduction upon you. Show me how you would bow to give him a subtle but effective cut direct . . ."

Two

Adalaide spent the next hour putting her newest pupil through his paces. As she'd already noted, he was most intelligent, and he took well to instruction. Still, there was something untamed and dangerous about him that had her questioning if he would ever truly fit into the rigid world of the *ton*.

"No, my lord, when you are making your bows to a lady, you must give every appearance of delight," she scolded, sending him a stern look. "Remember, you're being introduced to a charming and lovely young lady, not being presented to your executioner. Smile, Lord St. Jerome. Smile."

His dark gold brows met in a scowl. "I'm a man, Miss Terrington, not some puppet with a doltish smile painted upon my face. I smile when I wish it, and when I mean it."

"Then you must learn to mean it more often," Addy returned, refusing to be intimidated by his surly manner. She thought of reminding him of his duty to Wellington, but upon reflection decided against it. She might have need of such a ploy in the future, and if she used it now, it was certain to lose its effectiveness. Still, there had to be some way of bending him to her will.

"Pretend every lady you meet is the lady of your heart," she said, brightening as inspiration struck. "She is your true love, your very dream of femininity, the ideal by which you measure every other female and find her wanting. Show me how you would greet such a lady."

He said nothing at first, and she feared he was about to turn recalcitrant. Then his lips curved in a slow smile, and the deep green of his eyes took on a decidedly wicked sparkle. Before she could protest he was capturing her hand in his, his gaze holding hers in unspoken command as he raised it to his lips.

"Mo cridhe." He all but purred the words in a husky voice made all the more tantalizing by the deep burr of his native tongue. "I am enchanted to have found you at last." His mouth brushed over the back of her hand, the intimate touch bringing a hectic blush to her cheeks.

She cast her aunt a frantic glance, and was relieved to see the older lady had nodded off over her knitting. "Better, my lord, much better," she said, hastily withdrawing her hand and striving for nonchalance. "But kindly remember you may not kiss a lady's hand unless she has given you express permission to do so. We would not wish for you to be thought of as fast."

A slashing dimple made a surprising appearance in his lean cheek. "Ah, but if she was truly the lady of my heart, would not such permission be assumed?"

Addy would not let him see he had rattled her. "A *gentleman*"—she stressed the word firmly—"would never assume anything; especially where a lady is concerned. Still, you have done well enough for a first time. We shall work on it again tomorrow, after we have seen the tailor."

He stiffened warily. "What do you mean by that?"

"Your uniform, sir," she said, indicating his jacket with a wave of her hand. "That will do for informal afternoons or private visits, but you will be wanting a more extensive wardrobe if you wish to be accepted in the very best drawing rooms."

"I ken that," he said, thrusting his jaw forward in a pugnacious gesture that was becoming all too familiar, "but I do not see why it need concern you. 'Twas my understanding I should have the choosing of my own clothing, if nothing else."

Adalaide paused, realizing she needed to proceed with the greatest delicacy, else she would set the viscount's back up even more than she already had. Men were such delicate creatures, and nowhere were they more vulnerable than in their accursed pride.

"Of course you may have the choosing of your wardrobe, my lord," she said soothingly, offering him her most cajoling smile. "I merely thought that as you have been out of the country for a number of years, you would welcome the counsel of someone who is more *au courant* with fashion. I have assisted other gentlemen in this area, and I am generally held to have impeccable taste. You needn't fear I shall rig you out in something that wasn't in the first stare of respectability, I assure you."

He studied her briefly, and then gave a slow nod. "As you wish it," he said with the condescension worthy of a pasha. "And so long as you don't expect me to caper about like a fop, I've no objections. Wait," he added, frowning as if a sudden thought had just occurred to him. "No French fabrics."

Addy blinked in confusion. "I beg your pardon?"

"No French fabrics," he repeated. "I've lost too many men to their bullets to be putting gold in their pockets now. I'll wear good English cloth, or I'll wearing nothing at all."

The blunt pronouncement brought another stain of color to Addy's face. Later there would be time to chide him for making such indelicate remarks; at the moment, she had more pressing matters to address.

"Your patriotism does you credit, my lord," she began, "but you must understand *everyone* wears at least some French fabrics. Naturally we shall do our best to avoid it if it offends, but—"

He folded his arms across his chest, his expression resolute. "No French fabrics."

Having dealt with difficult and irrational males for the better part of her life, Addy knew when to press and when to retreat. "Very well, Lord St. Jerome," she said, shuddering to think how Monsieur Henri would react when she told him. "No French fabrics."

The rest of the lesson passed without incident, and then Addy gently awakened her aunt. She was about to ring for tea when Lord Hixworth appeared for his daily instruction. Her first inclination was to send him on his way, but upon reflection, she asked him to join them. It would do the diffident earl a world of good to be introduced to a man of St. Jerome's strong character, and he in turn could benefit from meeting the affable young gentleman.

While they were waiting for the tea to be served, she gave the two men the opportunity to become better acquainted. Upon learning he was newly returned from the Peninsula, Lord Hixworth gave St. Jerome an incredulous look.

"You served with Wellington?" he asked, sighing enviously. "But that is marvelous! What an honor it must have been!"

St. Jerome brushed back his dark blond hair, a cold, distant expression stealing over his countenance. "An honor, aye, that much I will grant," he said, his lips twisting in a bitter smile. "But you're wrong to think there is anything marvelous about a battle. There's nothing but death and horror to be found."

The younger man's smile wobbled at the harsh observation. "Have—have I given offense, my lord?" he asked, sounding perilously close to tears.

Addy was about to step forward to save the earl from further disgracing himself, but Lord St. Jerome merely shook his head.

"No, lad, you did not," he said with surprising gentleness. "And my apologies to you for snapping off your nose. Miss Terrington is a harsh taskmaster, and all of this drilling has left me feeling as if I've spent the day on the parade field." He cast her a teasing look and added, "If ever you tire of instructing gentlemen in the social graces, Miss Terrington, you might wish to write Wellington. The Army could make use of you."

Lady Fareham gave a delicate shudder. "I pray you do not say such things, my lord, for it will only encourage her. She is already too managing by half, and I despair of her ever making an eligible match. Or even an ineligible one," she added, giving a low titter of laughter.

Addy ignored her aunt, irritated by what she regarded as unwarranted criticism. "I do not consider it managing to be of service to others," she responded with a regal sniff. "I have been blessed with abundant intelligence and the wit to make use of it. What sense would it make for me to sit idly by and watch while those lacking these things bumble their way through life? It is my duty to be of what help to them I can."

"And 'tis a duty you perform with the greatest enthusiasm, I've noted," Lord St. Jerome said, astonishing her with his support. "My compliments to you. 'Twould seem the general has placed me in the most capable of hands."

Addy thanked him with coolness, although inside she was preening with delight. Over the years she'd received similar compliments from other pupils, and while she was always gratified to have her efforts acknowledged, she couldn't remember being more pleased by a student's praise. Perhaps it was because this particular student was so unlike any of the other gentlemen she'd had cause to meet, she decided, sliding him a measuring glance through her lashes.

While the others chatted, Addy studied her newest pupil. She was amazed to discover Lord St. Jerome could be quite charming when he put his mind to it. To be sure, his wasn't the cold, polished charm of a seasoned gentleman about town, but if the way Aunt Matilda was blushing and simpering was any indication, it was every bit as effective. Even Lord Hixworth benefited from the attention being shown him, blossoming as the viscount sought his advice on the matter of purchasing a horse.

"Of course Tatts is where you'll want to go for a proper mount," the earl said, his voice surprisingly firm as he sipped his tea. "Be happy to go with you, if you'd like. The traders are an honest enough lot, but they'll pluck you clean if they think you a Johnny Raw."

A hard smile touched the edges of the viscount's lips. "No one has taken me for a Johnny Raw in a great many years," he replied obliquely. "But your company should be most welcome, my lord. Thank you."

The two men made plans to meet the following Thursday, and then Hixworth was taking his leave. Aunt Matilda saw him out, leaving Addy alone with St. Jerome. Knowing she only had a few precious moments before her aunt returned, she turned at once to his lordship.

"Do you really mean to take possession of your house this afternoon?" she asked, thinking of the conversation she'd overheard between the viscount and his solicitors.

He gave a curt nod. "Aye. The sooner, the better."

"What of your cousin?"

"What of him?" he asked with obvious indifference. "If he minds his tongue and his temper, he is welcome to stay. If not . . ." He lifted his massive shoulders in a shrug.

Addy nibbled her lip. Although she usually didn't hesitate offering her pupils the benefit of her expertise, she knew enough of the viscount to know he would hardly welcome her advice. Still, she felt obliged to say something, lest he commit a social solecism.

"Do you think that wise?" she began cautiously. "Your cousin has been living in your uncle's house for some months now, and he may need time to secure other lodgings. A gentleman would offer his kinsman the shelter of his roof, regardless of the ill feelings between them."

As she expected, the viscount pokered up at once. "A gentleman did no' inherit the title," he informed her, his accent obvious in his displeasure. "I did."

"But, my lord, I—"

"Understand this, madam," he interrupted, sending her a warning glare. "I shall play the fine gentleman when it suits me, but when it does no', I shall be what I am; a soldier. And a soldier never surrenders ground so dearly won. What is mine I'll keep, and I'll hold it by whatever force necessary. You would do well to remember that."

Addy opened her lips to protest, but Lady Fareham chose that moment to return. "I do believe that is the most talkative I have ever seen Lord Hixworth," she observed, looking pleased. "Perhaps you are right, Adalaide, and there is some hope for the creature after all."

Addy was of no mind to discuss the earl, but unfortunately could think of no way to continue the argument with her aunt looking on in avid interest. And St. Jerome knew it too, she realized, noting the sharp gleam of awareness in his eyes.

"I fear I must be taking my leave as well," he said, offering each of them a low bow. "My solicitors are waiting for me, and I must be away. Pray accept my thanks for all the kindness you have shown me. I am in your debt."

The polite words were prosaic enough, but the way he

spoke them and the earnest expression on his face made Addy realize he was in earnest. Others might take their hospitality and think nothing of it, but the viscount was cut from a very different bolt of cloth. He did consider himself in their debt, and her ever nimble mind was quick to leap upon the fact.

"Don't forget we are to begin work on your wardrobe tomorrow," she said, eager to regain the control she acknowledged she'd lost. "Monsieur Henri shall be expecting us."

A crafty expression Addy could not like stole across his features. "As you have spent the past several days lecturing me on my duties and obligations, Miss Terrington, I am sure you must realize that a viscount does not wait upon a tailor; a tailor waits upon a viscount. Send Monsieur Henri to my house. I shall see him there."

"But my lord," Addy protested, annoyed he had proven to be so clever. "That will never do, as I am sure *you* must realize. If Monsieur Henri goes to your house, I couldn't possibly go with him. It would be most improper."

He raised an elegant eyebrow. "Would it?" he drawled, looking satisfied. "How sad. But do not fash yourself, Miss Terrington. I am sure we shall still be seeing a great deal of one another. Good day." And with that final bit of impertinence he walked out of the room, leaving a highly vexed Addy to glare after him in frustration.

* * *

"So the prodigal son has returned, or perhaps I should say, the prodigal nephew."

Mr. William Atherton lay sprawled in the elegant leather chair, a half-empty snifter of brandy cradled in his hand as he gazed drunkenly up at Ross. His cravat had been untied, and with his pale brown hair falling across his forehead, he looked every inch the debauched and indolent English gentleman Ross had come to loathe. Tossing him out into the street would be a pleasure.

"I must say I am surprised you've managed to survive all these years in his majesty's service," his cousin continued, not seeming to note Ross's rigid silence. "I gather it's true what they say: *Fortes fortuna juvat.* Fortune favors the brave."

"I am sorry to disappoint you, cousin," Ross replied, not bothering to inform him he spoke Latin. Let the pig think him an ignorant Scot. It could only serve to lull him into a false sense of superiority.

"Oh, I am not disappointed, Sergeant." Atherton sneered at Ross's rank. "Merely surprised, as I have said. Uncle would be in high alt did he know you were safely arrived in London. He lived in terror you would die in battle, and the title would then fall to me. He was quite proud of you, you know," he added, his dark gray eyes shining with enmity.

The artless confession took Ross aback, a fact he was careful to keep hidden. "Indeed?" he responded, wondering how much was art and how much fact. "I shouldn't have thought it, given the harsh words between us."

Atherton gave an ugly laugh and partook of a deep

gulp of brandy. "Oh, at first he was as angry as could be," he said, studying Ross with ill-disguised fury. "Brought me up from Devon, vowing he'd break the entitlement by whatever means necessary and make me his heir. Then he decided he rather fancied having a war hero as the next viscount, and I became redundant. He kept me close, mind, in the event you died for king and country, but there was no further mention of my being named his heir."

Ross said nothing, but stood silently assessing the potential danger his cousin posed. The man seemed harmless enough now, but Ross had the scars on his back to remind him how quickly a drunkard could turn violent when the mood was upon him.

"Nothing to say?" Atherton gave another laugh. "A taciturn lot, you Scots, and practical in the bargain. Daresay a title seemed a godsend to you, to say nothing of the fortune that came with it." He cocked his head to one side as if in consideration.

"Of course," he drawled, studying Ross mockingly, "you could always keep the title and sign the monies and properties not entailed over to me. But I suppose there's little chance of that, eh, cousin?"

Ross scowled, disliking the implication he was avaricious. "It makes no sense to keep the one and give away the other," he answered. He'd faced many enemies, in battle and in his own camp, and he knew that if he turned his back, his cousin would likely stick a knife in it. Not that he was worried. He could kill the *cladhaire* before he drew his next breath, if need be.

"Yes, that is what I thought you would say." Atherton downed the rest of the brandy before rising unsteadily to his feet. "Ah, well, can't fault a fellow for trying." He began weaving toward the door.

Ross watched him go, silently cursing Miss Terrington. The devil take the interfering and managing bluestocking, he thought, seething in resentment. She was right.

"Cousin, wait," he said, forcing the words through gritted teeth. "There's no need to leave. You may remain here, if you wish it."

Atherton paused at the door, swaying slightly. "And have it bruited about that I am living off your largesse?" he asked, sketching an elaborate bow that almost had him toppling over. "No, Sergeant, I thank you, but I have no need of your charity. Uncle may have seen fit to leave all to you, but I would not have you think I am completely without prospects. After all, I am *your* heir, am I not?"

Ross tensed in wariness. "Aye," he agreed coolly. "I would suppose that you are."

Atherton smirked. "If that will be all, Sergeant, I must be going. My friends are expecting me." He turned once more toward the door.

"Wait," Ross called out. "There is one thing more."

"Yes, Sergeant?"

Ross fixed the other man with his coldest stare. "I am the viscount now," he said, his tone none the less deadly for all its softness. "When you address me, you will use my title. Is that understood?"

An expression of naked hatred flashed across Atherton's face, and was quickly gone. "Of course, Lord St. Jerome," he said, inclining his head mockingly. "As you say."

After his cousin departed, Ross toured his new quarters. The house was small by London standards, but to Ross's eyes it seemed a veritable palace. It was hard to think one man should need so much space.

"Ten rooms?" he asked the regal individual who had introduced himself as McNeil, his uncle's, and now his, butler.

"Not including the kitchens and servants' quarters, my lord," McNeil replied, dabbing a speck of dust from a table with his snowy handkerchief. "The house in Surrey has nearly twice that number, and the northern properties have houses as well."

Ross said nothing, although his head spun at the thought of all he now owned. En route from Spain his uncle's solicitors had gone over his inheritance with him, but he'd been too ill for the information to impact him. Now that he'd had time to recover, he had a better understanding of his new circumstances, and it staggered him. He'd gone from a rough, battle-hardened soldier with little more than the clothes on his back to a titled lord with four expensive properties, literally overnight.

The reality of his new position might have overwhelmed another man, but he couldn't allow himself that luxury. However daunting the prospects before him might be, he had to succeed in the new role fate had handed him. Too many lives hung in the balance for him to be anything other than victorious.

With that thought firmly in mind, he turned his attention to securing his new holdings. Thinking in purely military terms, he concluded that as the enemy—his cousin—had held the ground first, it was wise to assume he'd left spies to report back to him. He wouldn't dismiss any of the staff unless he had proof they were in league with Atherton, but neither would he let them close enough to learn anything of value.

He dined that night in lonely and uncomfortable splendor, trying his best to eat all the food the butler kept placing before him. In the end he gave up with a groan, and retired to his rooms for the night. His valet, Joseph, was waiting for him, and Ross's plans for an early evening were firmly squelched when Joseph presented him with a list.

"What the devil is this?" Ross demanded impatiently, frowning as he recognized Miss Terrington's elegant script.

"A list of clothing Miss Terrington wishes you to order," Joseph said in the patient tones of one addressing a not overly bright child. "She has listed the fabrics and color of each item, and the number of each she thinks you will need. You are to review the list and add any articles which are missing. It will be presented to the tailor when he arrives tomorrow, that he might begin your new wardrobe at once."

Ross scanned the list, impatience giving way to incredulity. "Eight dozen handkerchiefs?" he demanded, raising his eyes to meet Joseph's bland gaze. "Who the bloody devil needs eight dozen handkerchiefs?"

"You do, my lord," Joseph replied primly. "And of finest lawn, please note. Should the occasion arise and you need to offer a handkerchief to a lady, it would not do to offer her something of inferior quality."

Ross stared at him for a moment, amazed to find himself fighting the urge to laugh. He had a sudden image of Miss Terrington, her pretty face set in stern disapproval, leaping out of the bushes and scolding him for offering some formless lady the wrong kind of handkerchief.

"No, I suppose it would not," he said, his voice carefully controlled. "What other orders did Miss Terrington send?" He knew his instructress too well to think she would content herself with one paltry list.

In answer Joseph reached into his pocket. "These are a review of what has already been covered," he said, handing Ross several sheets of paper. "And these"— more paper was proffered—"are a list of what will be covered in the next session. Have you any questions, my lord?"

Ross's lips twitched. "No, Joseph, I do not," he said, and then unable to contain himself, he threw back his head and roared with laughter. He'd thought his sergeant from his first days as a recruit was the toughest, most demanding creature on the face of God's green earth, but he was as innocent as a babe when compared to Miss Terrington.

He'd only been teasing when he suggested she offer her services to Wellington, but now he thought it might be just the thing. Given a few sergeants like her to whip the soldiers into shape, the earl would take Spain within the month. Given ten of her, Wellington would be in France by year's end. The thought had him chuckling as he settled on a chair to review his orders.

Three

The following afternoon a disgruntled Ross presented himself at Miss Terrington's. He'd spent the morning being poked at and insulted by the officious French tailor, and his temper was simmering like a pot about to boil over. Even the fact he was wearing a handsome new jacket and a pair of fashionable breeches the tailor had altered for him did little to soothe his ire, and by the time he arrived at Bruton Street he was spoiling for a brawl. His intentions to have it out with his tyrannical instructress, however, were thwarted when he walked into the elegant parlor and found her and her aunt holding court with the three gentlemen waiting there.

Miss Terrington glanced up at his arrival, a warm smile of welcome lighting her face as she rose to greet him.

"My lord, I am so glad you are come," she said, her blue eyes bright behind her spectacles. "Did things go well with Monsieur Henri? He can be a trifle difficult at times."

Ross thought of the despotic tailor and managed a grim smile. "I am an old hand at dealing with the

French, ma'am," he drawled in response, and because he could think of no reason not to, he caught the slender hand she'd offered him and raised it to his lips.

To his delight, her eyes widened in amazement, and a soft flow of rose washed across her cheeks. But even as he was savoring her response she was turning away, as efficient as always as she introduced him to the other occupants of the room.

" 'Tis all a tempest in a teacup, if you ask me," opined the Duke of Creshton, his bushy eyebrows meeting in a scowl. "Who in their proper mind would want to recall Wellington?"

"The Whigs, of course!" retorted the Earl of Denbury. "They've always been thick as inkleweavers with the Frogs, and they'd like nothing better than to see him back in England. Daresay he's pinned their ears back a time or two, eh, Sergeant?" He winked at Ross.

"A time or two, aye, my lord," Ross agreed, noting with interest the way the earl pronounced his rank, and the way his cousin had sneered it.

"Whoever may be behind the petition and their reasons for doing so is not at issue here," said the hard-eyed man who had been introduced as the Marquess of Falconer. "What matters is that they not succeed. Lord St. Jerome." His clear, golden gaze rested on Ross's face. "You were in a position to know his lordship in a way none of us ever could. As a soldier, what do you see as his greatest strength and his greatest weakness?"

"Be blunt if you will," he added, as if sensing Ross's hesitation. "You'll do England no good by saying only what you think we wish to hear."

Ross cast Miss Terrington a speculative glance before responding. In her pretty gown of yellow-and-cream-striped muslin, her red curls peeking out from beneath her starched cambric cap, she looked every inch the proper Society lady. He'd have thought such a creature would find the conversation singularly boring, but if her avid expression was any indication, she was as interested in his reply as any of the men. Her reaction surprised him, and he wondered if all women of her class were equally as intrigued by the matter. Probably not. Miss Terrington struck him as being an *un*typical lady of any class.

"Wellington's greatest strength is as a strategist," he said at last, granting his listeners the courtesy of complete honesty. "He fights hard for the most advantageous ground, and he holds it fast once he's won it. He also makes excellent use of cover, and he's careful not to squander his troops uselessly. An important consideration from a common soldier's perspective," he added with a shrug.

"And his greatest weakness?" Lord Falconer pressed.

That took a little more thought. "I've met the general but the one time," he continued cautiously. "But he strikes me as a man, like any other. Hard, shrewd, a wee bit proud, perhaps, but he is a man I or any other soldier in Spain would follow into hell did he ask it of us."

A satisfied look flashed across the marquess's face. "I can think of no higher endorsement. Thank you, my lord."

A heated debate followed, and Ross was amused to observe that the art of politics was fought every bit as hard as the art of warfare. Strategy, the marshaling of troops and resources, and the judicious use of intelligence counted as much in the ballroom as on the battlefield, with the participants far less nice in their notions. Both Lady Fareham and Miss Terrington contributed to the discussion, with Miss Terrington showing a not unexpected talent for subterfuge.

In the end it was agreed the sooner Ross made his bows, the better. Given the fact he was one of London's most eligible bachelors, Lord Falconer would be the one to introduce Ross to Society, ably seconded by Lords Denbury and Creshton. His first public appearance would be tomorrow evening at the home of Creshton's heir, who was celebrating his recent wedding.

"It's the perfect occasion," the duke assured him with a wink. "Small enough not to be a dashed squeeze, but large enough to make certain everyone you'll need to meet will be there."

"An excellent suggestion, your grace," Miss Terrington approved with a brisk nod. "Although this means we shall have to work doubly hard if we are to be ready in time. His lordship has done quite well, but there are still several things he will need to learn before engaging the enemy."

Ross said nothing, although 'twas hard. He was accustomed to being addressed by his commanding officers as if he were a brainless dolt, but that didn't mean he cared for the sensation. His word to Wellington aside, there were limits to his patience, and Miss Terrington had just reached those limits. It seemed 'twas time he and the diminutive tyrant came to an understanding. Tamping down his emotions, he settled back in his chair, sipping his tea and waiting with unholy patience for the coming battle.

"That went rather well," Addy said, smiling at Lord Falconer as she and her aunt escorted the three gentlemen from the room. "His grace is a notorious high stickler, and the fact he is willing to sponsor Lord St. Jerome is certain to count in his favor, don't you agree?"

"If you say so, Miss Terrington."

The cool reply had Addy frowning. The aloof marquess had never been loquacious, but she'd never known him to be quite so taciturn. Puzzled, she shot him a quick glance, and was surprised to find him watching her with icy disapproval.

"Is something amiss, my lord?" she asked, casting about in her mind for whatever she might have done to give offense.

His golden gaze, sharp and deadly as the bird of prey for which he was named, met hers with a jolt of power. "Should there be?" he queried softly.

Addy scowled in annoyance. "*I* do not believe so," she shot back, losing all patience, "but 'tis plain you do! Cut line, sir, and tell me precisely what you mean."

There was a pause as he continued studying her. "I am sure you mean well," he said at last. "And I am equally sure Lord St. Jerome is grateful for your pains, but you go too far when you reprimand him in front of others. Mind you don't do so again."

"What are you talking about?" Addy demanded with genuine outrage. "I am certain I did no such thing!"

"Did you not?" he challenged. "Somehow I doubt his lordship would agree."

Addy shifted under an unexpected stab of conscience. She supposed some unenlightened souls might consider her behavior toward St. Jerome as a *trifle* high-handed, but in her defense, she didn't treat his lordship any differently than she treated her other students. She was the teacher, after all, and they the pupils; a certain amount of despotism was expected, necessary even, if she was to accomplish her tasks. And yet . . .

"I suppose I might have waited until we were alone to speak with him," she said, conceding her guilt with sulky reluctance. "My apologies, sir, if I have given offense."

Falconer raised a jet-black eyebrow. "I am not the one to whom your apology is owed," he responded. "But if you wish St. Jerome to accept your pretty words, might I suggest you offer them with a great deal more honesty than you offered them to me? Good day, Miss Terrington." He followed the others out the door.

"Such a handsome young man," Aunt Matilda enthused, sighing after his departing figure. "A pity he is so cold."

Addy merely grumbled in response. She would like to pretend the marquess was wrongheaded, but her innate honesty would not let her lie. However comfortable it might be to think otherwise, she knew she owed her pupil an apology. The question remained. How to go about it and still maintain the upper hand? She thought for a moment, and then turned to her aunt.

"Aunt, would you wait in the hall for a few minutes?" she asked, laying a restraining hand on the older woman's arm. "I should like to speak privately with his lordship, if you please."

"Apologize to him, you mean," Lady Fareham corrected, looking pleased. "Good. I should have rung a peal over your head had you not. You shamed us all with your shocking want of conduct, and I expect you to beg his lordship's forgiveness. I shall give you ten minutes, no more. Mind you make proper use of them."

Addy bit back a most unladylike sentiment before turning resolutely toward the door. She took a moment to compose herself, straightened her spectacles, and then stepped back into the parlor. Lord St. Jerome was standing in front of the fireplace, and he glanced over his shoulder at her arrival.

"Miss Terrington," he began, his tones as rigid as his posture. "There is something I should like to say to you. Be so good as to close the door."

Addy complied with a touch more force than was necessary. Years of dealing with males had taught her that the best way of handling confrontations was head-on. Men expected women to demur and prevaricate, and it always took them aback to be straightforward and use logical discourse.

"If you mean to ring a peal over my head, sir, I should advise you to save your breath," she said with a deliberate air of injured pride. "Lord Falconer and Aunt have already done so."

He jerked back his head, and she felt a sense of triumph as the anger in his eyes gave way to wary surprise. "Have they?" he asked, his husky voice filled with suspicion.

"And very effectively too," she said, settling her skirts

about her as she resumed her seat. "Aunt was especially eloquent in her disapproval, and I assure you I am most thoroughly cowed."

He regarded her closely. "You do not appeared cowed to me," he observed. "Sullen, mayhap, and bad-tempered, but I shouldn't call you cowed."

"Then you would be mistaken, my lord," she returned, meeting his gaze with what equanimity she could gather. "I have been made to see the error of my ways, and I apologize if my incautious remarks offended you. Such was never my intention."

He settled in the chair facing hers, an expression she could not decipher on his handsome countenance. "Let me see if I have the right of this," he began in careful tones. "You treat me like a brat still in leading strings, insult my intelligence, and then tell me you mean no offense. Is that correct?"

"Yes," she said, sensing a trap but not certain how to avoid it. "And now that I think on it, I fail to see why you are so upset. I should have that as a soldier, you would be more accustomed to taking orders."

"And so I am, but as you're always reminding me, I'm not a soldier now. I am the viscount, and a viscount, I'm thinking, would not take so well to such summary commands."

Addy considered that for a moment, and realized she had been condemned by her own words. "Perhaps not," she said, grudgingly acknowledging his point. "But—"

"Miss Terrington." He leaned forward, a look of hard determination stamped on his face. "For me to succeed in the role General Wellington has assigned me, 'tis imperative I have the respect of the men I shall be meeting.

And how can I have that when you've made it plain you don't respect me?"

She couldn't have been more stunned had he reached out and slapped her. "I do respect you, Lord St. Jerome! How can you say I do not?"

In answer he began listing every comment and correction she'd made during the brief meeting. By the time he finished, she was gaping at him in astonishment.

"But I do that to all my pupils!" she exclaimed, amazed a battle-hardened solider should prove to be so sensitive. "If I don't correct them privately, then they are certain to blunder publicly. And believe me, Society is a far harsher critic than I could ever hope to be!"

"Of that I have no doubt," he agreed, "but my point is you didn't reprimand me in private. You did so in front of the three men whose support is vital to this mission, and in doing that, you may well have jeopardized everything."

"What nonsense! You—"

"Listen to me," he interrupted, closing his hand about her wrist. " 'Tis not my own pride I'm thinking of. For myself, I don't give a tinker's curse what you or any man may think of me. But for Wellington, for the men in Spain fighting and dying, I cannot be so indifferent. If society laughs at me, if they take me for the untutored dunce you treat me, then I should have failed my mission, and I would die rather than do that. Do you understand now what you have risked with your shrew's tongue?"

To Addy's horror, she could feel a painful lump forming in her throat. "I'm sorry, my lord," she whispered, and this time she meant every word. "I am so very sorry."

"I am sure that you are," St. Jerome continued, relentless as a judge, "but it makes no difference. Had those men not been so firmly in Wellington's corner, only think of the mischief they might have made. I should have been the laughingstock of London, and all of this would have been for naught."

"Then what are you suggesting?" Addy asked, trying to follow his convoluted logic. "Are you saying I should just turn you loose upon Society as you are?"

"I am saying no such thing," he returned, releasing her arm and leaning back in his chair. "I agree I am still in want of instructing, and when we are private, you may treat me however ill you please. Curse me, strike me, break a pot over my head if that is what it takes to drive a lesson home, and I'll not say a word. But when others are about, you will treat me with the same respect and courtesy you would show any other lord."

"No, wait." He paused, surprising her with a smile. "Allow me to amend that. I've seen the way you treat poor Hixworth. What I meant is you'll treat me as a lord who hasn't the misfortune of being under your thumb; with all the respect and courtesy you'd show Wellington himself. Are we agreed?"

It made sense, and Addy rather liked the part about breaking a pot over his head. It sounded promising. If she took his meaning, she was free to terrorize him however much she pleased in the confines of their classroom. Outside it she had but to bridle her tongue, and upon reflection that didn't sound so very difficult. She was even courteous to that dolt Cousin Teddy when put to the sticking point. How much easier would it be to show a man she actually esteemed the required deference?

"As you wish, my lord," she said, straightening her shoulders and meeting his gaze with a lift of her chin. "Now, if you are done making me grovel, I will ring for my aunt. Unless you've some objection?" She lifted an eyebrow in arrogant inquiry.

His lordship's lips twitched, but his voice was impassive as ever. "No, Miss Terrington, I've no objections."

Addy knew a faint sensation of relief, which she quickly brushed aside. "Very well, then, we shall begin anew. If you are to make your bows in a little over twenty-four hours, we've much to accomplish. I note you are quite good at rational conversation, but as rational conversation in Society constitutes a contradiction in terms, we must see that you develop a proper well of small chat. Tell me, my lord, how do you find the weather in London this time of year?"

It was Lady Fareham who thought of dancing.

"You do dance, my lord, don't you?" she demanded, eying Ross through her lorgnette. "It is a requirement of all gentlemen that they conduct themselves gracefully upon the dance floor."

"No, my lady, I do not dance," Ross replied, his head aching from all the knowledge being stuffed into it. His face was also stiff from the fatuous smile he'd been holding for what seemed like forever, and his nerves were stretched to the fraying point. He felt like a choice worm being pecked to death by a pair of voracious hens, and had he been less a soldier, he'd have fled the field hours ago.

"But this is dreadful!" Miss Terrington said, frowning at him in patent disapproval. "All young blades dance. How can it be you've never learned?"

"Perhaps because I'm no' a young blade," Ross reminded her, rubbing his head. "And as for never learning, you forget I've been in Spain for the past four years. With whom should I have danced? The other soldiers?"

His sarcasm was wasted on his instructress. "No, I suppose that would not have done," she agreed, looking thoughtful. "However would you have decided which of you would lead? Ah well", she paid no mind to his sputtering, "we shall simply have to take care of the matter ourselves. Aunt" . . . she turned an expectant gaze upon Lady Fareham . . . "if you would be so kind?"

At first Ross thought the older lady meant to partner him, and was surprised when she went to the pianoforte sitting in the corner and settled in front of the keys.

"Now then." Miss Terrington was smiling up at him. "As this is to be a dinner ball, there will only be a handful of sets before and after dinner. Most of the steps are fairly similar, and once you've mastered them you should have no trouble learning the others. We shall begin with a contradance."

The remaining part of the afternoon was spent learning a bewildering set of steps that left Ross feeling as awkward as a plow horse in a parlor. Fortunately he'd been ever fond of music, and he found that by concentrating on the lilting notes and matching Miss Terrington's graceful moves, he was able to give a good accounting of himself. When he completed an entire set without a misstep, Miss Terrington pronounced herself satisfied with his efforts.

"Of course we must see that you learn the other fashionable dances as the Season goes on," she said, her soft cheeks flushed from exertion. "But this is a very good start; a very good start indeed. Do you not agree, Aunt?"

"The lad did very well," Lady Fareham replied, nodding approvingly at Ross. "He's near as graceful as Hixworth, and not half so clumsy as that fool Benchton. He broke your poor foot, as I recall it."

"Only a toe," Miss Terrington said with a casual shrug, "and he was so apologetic, I really could not hold it against him."

"You have taught other men to dance?" Ross demanded. He didn't know why it should be so, but the notion of her teaching another man what she had just spent hours teaching him was faintly shocking.

"Of course," she replied, giving him a patient look. "Dancing is as much a part of my curriculum as learning to bow and the correct way to handle a team. Which reminds me; when you go to Tattersall's with Lord Hixworth, mind you purchase yourself a curricle and some cattle as well as a mount. I mean to have Lord Falconer recommend you for the Four-in-Hand Club."

"What the devil is that?"

"A club for foolish young men with more gold than good sense," Lady Fareham answered with a sniff. "They like to racket about London frightening women and overturning other carriages with their poor driving, and then call it sport. But if you want to be taken as *un homme du monde,* it is necessary that you be accepted as one of them."

Ross rather fancied being taken as a man of the world, but he wasn't as certain he wanted to join such a club. The members sounded too much like the bored and careless young officers he'd encountered on the Peninsula, who saw racing as just another way to get themselves killed between battles. He'd seen one such young man run down a Portuguese child, and only stop to make certain his horse hadn't suffered an injury. No, he didn't want to be taken for such a man.

"Lord Falconer belongs to this club?" he asked, surprised the other man should participate in something so frivolous.

"Oh, yes, the marquess is a noted whipster," Miss Terrington said, crossing the room to ring for tea. "He also boxes at Gentleman Jackson's Salon and shoots at Manton's Gallery, where he's counted such a deadly shot none will challenge him. Indeed, if he weren't so neat in his appearance and so somber in his demeanor, I daresay he'd be labeled a Corinthian."

A Corinthian. Ross mentally reviewed the dictionary Miss Terrington had prepared for him, giving the words Society used, and listing their precise meaning. A Corinthian was a sports-mad young man who fancied going about looking and behaving like a drunken coachman; a ridiculous occupation, or so Ross thought. Then a more horrifying thought occurred to him.

"*I'll* not have to be a Corinthian, will I?" he demanded, appalled at the very possibility.

"Of course not." Miss Terrington looked equally horrified.

Ross relaxed with a relieved sigh. "Thank heaven for that."

"You're far too old to be a Corinthian, although we might want to pass you off as a rake. Rakes do so much better in Society, do you not think so, Aunt?"

"So long as they don't go about seducing the wrong young ladies," Lady Fareham concurred. "But are you quite sure you want him to be taken for a rake, Adalaide? I thought you wished him to be viewed as a serious young lord anxious to do his duty."

The two women continued discussing the coming Season and the role he would be expected to play; never once bothering to seek his opinion. Ross listened in stony silence, bitterly accepting how little choice he had in their decision. The admission was hurtful, and for a moment he was thrown back into the past and facing his uncle's solicitor across his father's coffin.

"Of course you will come to London, Mr. Mac-Cailan," the older man had told him, studying him over a pair of spectacles. "You are your uncle's heir, and your proper place is at his side. We shall depart after the services."

In crude English and even cruder Gaelic Ross had told him what he thought of such a plan. Not even the promise of the commission he had longed for was enough to change his mind, and when the solicitor had been so incautious as to make vague threats, Ross had thrown him out of the kirk. He'd been twenty then, and full of pride and determination. Fourteen hard and bloody years later, he now found himself right where his uncle had wanted him. It looked as if the old *aintighearna* had had the final laugh after all.

Impatient with his unhappy memories, Ross rose abruptly to his feet, almost upsetting the tea cart in his haste.

"I beg your pardon, Lady Fareham, Miss Terrington," he said, voice raw with the emotion tearing through him. "But I must go. I shall return on the morrow." He began striding purposefully toward the door.

"But what is wrong, my lord?" Miss Terrington demanded, gazing at him in a mixture of alarm and annoyance. "Are you ill? Shall I send for the doctor?"

Ross shook his head. "No, that is not necessary. I just recalled a previous engagement, and I must be away else I shall be shockingly late. Good day." And he fled the room before his instructress could stop him.

"Well, and what was that all about, do you think?" Aunt Matilda asked, gazing at Addy in confusion. "The poor lad dashed out of here as if his breeches were afire."

"I am sure I do not know," Addy said, wondering if she should give chase. She knew his lordship denied being ill, but she was too well acquainted with men to give his denial any credence. Most men she knew would sooner die than admit to an infirmity, and as she'd already learned to her cost, Lord St. Jerome had twice the pride of any man she'd ever met. Perhaps she would have the doctor call upon him regardless, she decided, nibbling worriedly on her lip. It wouldn't do for the viscount to suffer a relapse at some inopportune moment.

She and her aunt settled back to finish their tea, and

she was considering retiring to her rooms for the afternoon when there was a tap on the door and Williams entered the room.

"I beg pardon, my lady, Miss Terrington," he said stiffly. "But there is a gentleman outside who insists upon seeing you. He gave me his card and asked that I present it to you." He offered the silver tray and the card upon it with an expression of rigid censure on his imperious features.

Intrigued, Addy accepted the card, her eyebrows raising as she recognized the name stamped on the fine parchment.

"How very interesting," she said, handing the card to her aunt. "Very well, Williams, please show Mr. Atherton in."

Williams sniffed, a clear sign he disapproved of their guest. He returned a few moments later, an elegantly attired gentleman trailing in his wake. The gentleman made his bows first to Lady Fareham and then to Addy, his manner polished and only a trifle condescending as he took his seat.

"I thank you ladies for being so good as to receive me when we've not been formally introduced," Mr. Atherton said, simpering at them each in turn. "You may make certain I should never have done so were matters not so grave. It is about my cousin."

"Lord St. Jerome?" Addy said, instantly alarmed. It had been less than half an hour since the viscount had taken his hasty leave; surely he couldn't have collapsed so soon?

"Is he all right?" she demanded, cursing herself for

not seeking medical assistance for him when she had the chance.

Mr. Atherton's unremarkable features twisted into a sneer. "As to that, I am not certain how to answer," he said with an ugly laugh. "He was hale and hearty the last I saw of him. He was throwing me from my house at the time."

Addy thought it impolite to remind her visitor the house was the legal property of St. Jerome. "I am sorry to hear that, Mr. Atherton," she said, adopting her most brisk manner, "but what do you mean, you've come about your cousin? Explain yourself, if you please."

In response he leaned back in his chair, his dark gray eyes studying her with a boldness that bordered on insolence. "One hears such interesting things these days," he drawled. "It is being bruited about that you've set yourself up as some sort of tutor for gentlemen, and that you are even now instructing my loutish cousin in the refined arts. Is that true?"

"It is true I have offered some gentlemen of my acquaintance the benefit of my expertise, but I am not so toplofty as to consider myself a tutor," Addy responded carefully, deciding she didn't care for the man's mocking tone nor his slighting reference to the viscount. "May I ask how this concerns you?"

He answered her question with one of his own. "And how much do you charge for this . . . expertise, if I may ask?"

Aunt Matilda gave an outraged screech and she leapt to her feet. "Sir! You will leave this house at once!" she shrilled, pointing at the door with a shaking finger. "I will not have my niece insulted by a . . . a rake and a rattle!"

Addy also rose, but it was not indignation or fear that had her hands shaking. It was pure and simple fury.

"No, Aunt, I will answer Mr. Atherton's question, and then we shall have Williams toss him out," she said, her narrowed gaze resting on the man, who remained sprawled in his chair.

"I charge nothing for aiding others, sir," she told him, making no effort to mask the contempt she felt. "I consider it my duty to be of what help I can, although in your cousin's case, my help is hardly needed."

"Indeed?" Atherton replied, the look of cold enmity in his eyes belying his affected drawl. "And why is that?"

"Because he is already three times the gentleman you could ever hope to be," Addy retorted, taking the greatest pleasure in watching the fatuous smile fade from her visitor's lips. "Now leave this house."

"Of course, Miss Terrington," he murmured, rising to his feet with insulting slowness. "And pray forgive me if I have offended. It appears I was operating under a misapprehension. I took you for a woman of intellect who would listen to reason, but it seems you are no more clever than the rest of your sex. Pity. We might have been friends." And with a final, mocking bow, he took his leave.

"Insolent villain!" Aunt Matilda was beside herself with fury. "You ought to have boxed his ears for him, Adalaide, instead of letting him strut out of here like a rooster. The nerve of the wretch! Well"—she sat back down and picked up her teacup—"we shall see what Lord St. Jerome has to say about this! I am sure he can be counted upon to take that scoundrel down a peg or two."

"Which is precisely why we shan't tell him," Addy replied, realizing somewhat belatedly the game the repellent Mr. Atherton had been playing. She'd thought it odd he should seek her out so quickly, but now she understood. The man was out to make a scandal, and she was hanged if she would help him.

"Not tell him?" Her aunt was gaping at her as if she'd taken leave of her senses. "But Adalaide. . . ."

"I mean it, Aunt." Addy gave the older woman her most forbidding stare. "Not one word about this to his lordship or anyone else. Lord Wellington has entrusted me with the task of making the viscount the most eligible man in London, and I can hardly do that if he hangs for his cousin's murder."

"Oh, dear, I hadn't thought of that," Lady Fareham replied, frowning thoughtfully. "But you are right, of course. We can't endanger your mission with a slight case of murder, however well deserved. Still"—her frown deepened as she raised the cup of tea to her lips—"it goes against the grain to let that unpleasant little man skip away unscathed after enduring his insults and innuendoes."

A slow smile curved Addy's lips. "Who said anything about his skipping away unscathed?"

An equally evil smile touched Lady Fareham's lips as she studied Addy's expression. "Like that, is it? Good. Only mind you don't get caught. The scandal will be none the less shocking if 'tis you who ends dangling at the end of the hangman's rope. Bury the bodies deep, that's my creed. Now about Almack's, dearest, are you quite sure you wish to take the viscount there? Poor boy, he's only just back from the Peninsula. Hasn't he suffered enough for king and country?"

Four

Refusing the butler's offer to summon a hack, Ross set out from the Terringtons' afoot. He walked without direction or purpose, his only intent to put as much distance as possible between himself and his demons. A chilly rain was falling, but he paid it little mind. He'd marched and fought in far worse conditions to be troubled by a bit of damp, and in any case, the physical discomfort he was feeling was far preferable to the anguish of his own thoughts.

The elegance of Mayfair gave way to the narrowed streets and cramped buildings of Holborn, and with each street he passed the crowds grew rougher and more dangerous. Distracted as he was, Ross had been too long a soldier not to be aware of his surroundings, and he knew the moment the two men emerged from the alleyway to close ranks behind him. He realized they were looking to rob him, and the possibility had him smiling in grim satisfaction. He'd been feeling the urge to tear something apart, and a nice, bloody brawl held unexpected appeal.

He continued strolling as if oblivious to the two footpads trailing him. In his current black mood he was of a mind to toy with his prey as he'd once toyed with the French; letting them think themselves the victor until he'd guide them into a trap from which there was no escape. Acting the ignorant nob, he led his pursuers up one filthy street and down another, until he wearied of the game. When he reached a street wide enough to offer space to fight and the means to escape should it prove necessary, he came to an abrupt halt.

Glancing about as if to get his bearings, he left himself seemingly open to attack. His pursuers were quick to take advantage, moving forward to box Ross between them. Both carried cudgels, and they tapped them against the palms of their grimy hands.

"Lost, are ye?" The heavier man asked, moving behind Ross while the other stepped in front of him, blocking his path. "We'd be 'appy ter 'elp ye find yer way agin, wouldn't we, Jimms?"

"More 'n 'appy," the man called Jimms confirmed, taking in Ross's elegant attire with obvious derision. "And while we're about it, we'd be 'appy ter relieve ye of that 'eavy purse yer carryin'. Give over, guv, and p'rhaps we'll let ye live."

Ross regarded them in silence. The gold he was carrying meant nothing to him, but that didn't mean he intended handing it over without a fight.

"You've mistaken your targets, lads," he advised them softly. "I'm no plump chicken to be so easily plucked. Leave now, and perhaps *I* shall let *you* live."

Jimms looked startled, and then pleased. "Yer choice, mate," he said, moving toward Ross, his cudgel raised.

Ross waited until the small club began its descent before making his move. Instead of trying to dodge the blow he stepped into it, catching Jimms's arm and twisting it until the other man howled in pain. He doubled his other hand into a fist, slamming it into the center of the thief's pudgy belly. Jimms folded with a strangled gasp, and in an instant Ross had scooped up his cudgel and was facing the other man.

"Come on," he invited, twirling the crude staff expertly. "You wanted my gold so badly; come and get it."

The remaining thief wasted little time with words. He dropped the cudgel and pulled out a knife, his dark eyes hot with fury as he faced Ross. "Bloody swell," he snarled, dropping into a fighter's stance. "I'll cut yer 'eart out!"

Ross leapt out of the way, easily avoiding the attack. The fight was short, but decisive. The other man was accustomed to back alley ambushes and taking on prey far weaker than himself, and he proved no match for a warrior of Ross's ability. In less than a minute Ross had disarmed him and was pressing him against the wall of a building, the blade of the thief's knife resting dangerously against the man's own throat.

"Now," Ross drawled, smiling, "the question is do I kill you, or do I let you go? If I release you, you'll only practice your villainy on some other poor sot. Perhaps I should just . . ." He applied the slightest bit of pressure, nicking the man's skin.

"No!" The thief cried, his eyes rolling in terror. "Let me go! We meant no 'arm! Just tryin' to make a livin' is all. Wot's it to ye, eh? Ye've more'n gold enough."

Ross was about to debate the point, when he saw the man's gaze shift over his left shoulder. That was the only warning he needed, and he spun around in time to pre-vent Jimms from dashing a brick over his head. Instead of striking his skull the blow landed on Ross's shoulder, sending a numbing pain shooting down his arm. He lashed out with his foot, sending the thief crashing to the ground, clutching his privates and retching in agony.

Parrying the attack left his back unguarded, and his opponent struck a brutal blow to Ross's kidneys. The pain drove Ross to his knees, but he kept a firm hold on the knife. He was struggling to draw breath, when he heard a voice cry out.

"Away, lads, away! The Charlie is a'comin'!"

The two thieves made their escape as best they could, pausing only long enough to give Ross a pun-ishing kick before disappearing into a nearby alley. Mindful he was still deep in enemy territory, Ross fought his way to his feet. He'd only partially achieved his goal when a shabbily dressed man knelt beside him.

"All right, sir?" he asked, gazing down at Ross in concern.

"Fine, I thank you," Ross managed through clenched teeth, In truth he was in agony, but he wasn't about to admit as much. Instead he blocked his mind to the pain, accepting the hand the man offered him as he rose some-what unsteadily to his feet.

"In the Army, was you?" his rescuer asked, eying Ross with rueful respect. "You fight like a man what's seen action."

"The Rifles," Ross responded, wincing as he bent to retrieve the hat he'd lost in the struggle. "You?"

"Fifty-second Foot," the man replied. "Or I was." He

touched the empty sleeve pinned to the front of his faded uniform. "Salamanca."

Ross nodded in understanding. "We lost many good men that day," he said, remembering the aftermath of the horrific battle.

"You'll get no argument from me," the man agreed, moving away from Ross. "From now on mind where you wander; Spain's a paradise compared to this stew. Good day to you, Captain." He turned to leave.

"Wait." Ross laid a restraining hand on the man's shoulder.

His rescuer whirled around. "If it's money you're offering, you may go to the devil!" he cried, his thin face twisting with pride. "I'm no beggar to be taking a rich man's coin!"

Ross hesitated, uncertain how to continue. He'd been about to offer the other man the entire contents of his purse, but now he could see it would not do. Had their situations been reversed, he knew he would also have tossed anything smacking of charity back in the other man's face; regardless of how empty his pockets might be. He studied the faded chevrons still proudly pinned on the other man's sleeve, and came to a swift decision.

"You may be at ease, Corporal," he said, meeting the man's wary glare. " 'Twas not money I was offering, but a position. I am need of another valet, and you look as if you'd be a good man to have about. Interested?"

A dozen different emotions flashed across the corporal's face. "A valet? What would I know about being a gentleman's gentleman?" he sneered, the derision in his voice not quite disguising the disbelieving hope shining in his eyes.

"About as much as I know about being a gentleman, I've no doubt," Ross returned lightly, a sense of peace stealing over him. "But I am learning, Corporal, and so can you."

"But Captain—"

Ross held up a hand. "You mistake my rank," he said, softening his objections with a smile. "Like you I was a *real* soldier; a sergeant. Now, do you wish the position, or do you not?"

The corporal's jaw dropped in amazement. *"You* was a sergeant?"

"Aye, Sergeant Ross MacCailan, at your service, sir," Ross said, offering the other man his hand. "And who have I the honor of addressing?"

"Nevil Collier," the corporal responded, accepting Ross's hand in dazed shock. "But I don't understand. How can a gent like you be a common soldier?" He scowled in sudden suspicion. "Not running some rig, are you? If you are, I'll have no part of it. I'm an honest man."

"As am I," Ross assured him. "I am also a gentleman, a viscount, to be precise, although I trust you'll not be holding that against me."

"No, Sergeant—my lord, I mean," Collier said, clearly at a loss. "But I don't see as why you'd be hiring me. It's not as if I can tie a cravat with this." He held up his hand in emphasis.

"There's no need for you to do that, as I already have a man to act in that capacity," Ross answered calmly. "Rather than a valet, what I really need is an aide-de-camp, a man I can trust to help guard my back. And if you think 'tis charity I am offering," he added, "you may think again. I was a damned hard sergeant, and I'll likely make a damned hard master. But look at it this way, Collier. If you have enough of me, you can always resign your post without fear of the firing squad."

A cautious grin crept across Collier's face. "Aye," he agreed, "there's always that."

"Then you'll accept?" Ross asked, waiting for his answer. His offer of employment had been made to spare the corporal's pride, but now he was determined that the other man accept. Not just for Collier's sake, he realized, but for his own sake as well.

"Aye," Collier said again, giving a wry chuckle. "I reckon I will. Provided you answer one question."

"And what might that be?"

Collier rocked back on his heels and surveyed Ross with amused skepticism. "How the devil did a sergeant in the bleeding Rifles get to be a viscount?"

The weight Ross had been carrying for the past several days slipped away, and he grinned in response. "That, Corporal, is a very long story," he said, slapping his hand on Collier's shoulder. "Come home and share a pint with me while I'm telling it."

In between fuming over Mr. Atherton's insults and brooding over St. Jerome's precipitous departure, Addy passed a restless night.

This wasn't the first time a pupil had fled her presence, but in the viscount's case she thought there was more to it than the usual fits of pique that had sent the others scrambling. His lordship was far too seasoned a soldier to desert his post without cause, and there had been something in his green eyes that left her feeling decidedly uneasy. It hadn't been fear or even anger she'd glimpsed, but rather a sense of almost raw desperation. Whatever his cause for leaving, it hadn't been for something as innocuous as a previous engagement, and she vowed to get to the bottom of the matter at their next meeting. With so much at stake, she couldn't allow anything to distract her pupil from his mission.

She was brooding over her possible courses of action when she walked into her study and found St. Jerome at his customary place before the fire. She gaped at him a full second before closing the door behind her and rushing to his side.

"My lord, what are you doing here?" she demanded, anxiously scanning him for any sign of illness or injury.

A blond eyebrow lifted in inquiry as he rose to his feet. "And where else would I be, Miss Terrington?" he asked, offering her a low bow. "My presentation is this very night, and as you are always reminding me, we've much to accomplish. Where shall we start?"

Addy's concern dissolved into temper. "You may start, sir, by explaining what you meant by dashing out of here yesterday afternoon!" she snapped, furious with herself for giving the wretch a moment's thought. "Were you still in the Army, you should have been shot for desertion!"

"So I would have," he agreed, his voice giving away nothing. "And for that you have my apology, and my assurance it shall not happen again. Now, if you are done dressing me down, shall we begin?"

Addy glared at him for several seconds before taking her seat. "You might have at least offered token resistance," she grumbled, settling her skirts about her. "There's no fun to be had in storming a citadel that has already surrendered."

"You mistake me, ma'am," he answered, resuming his seat. "I was not surrendering. I was accepting culpability for my sins. I have never surrendered, nor will I ever."

The fact that she admired him for the admission didn't mean Addy intended letting such an arrogant boast slip past unchallenged. She pulled down her spectacles and peered at him over the rims.

"Might I remind your lordship that pride goeth before a fall? I should take care against uttering such boastful words unless you are prepared to eat them."

"Now," she said, not giving him the chance to protest, "let us review. His grace will be performing the introductions this evening, and you're to take your cues from him. If he says he is 'delighted' to present you to a certain gentleman, it will mean that man is an ally of Wellington's, and you may rely upon him for assistance. However, if he allows he is merely 'pleased' to introduce someone, that man has aligned himself with the general's enemies and you're not to waste your time with him. And if he pronounces himself 'charmed—' "

"It means the man he is about to present has yet to declare himself, and I am to secure his support at all costs," St. Jerome finished with a nod. "Aye, Miss Terrington, I understand, but I think you and Creshton have the wrong of it."

"The wrong of what?" Addy demanded, piqued he should find fault with the code she and the others had spent several hours concocting.

"With showing Wellington's enemies the back of me,"

he replied coolly. "Were the general here, he would tell you that you never turn your back on an enemy in a fight. If you cannot destroy him, then you'd best be after winning him to your side."

"Indeed?" Addy sat back in her chair, much struck by the observation. "I should have thought it better sense to keep one's enemies as far from one as possible."

A feral grin touched St. Jerome's lips, making him look like the battle-hardened soldier he was. "A misconception, Miss Terrington. In a battle you want your enemy always in front of you, where you know where he is and what he is about."

"What of the enemies you have won to your side?" Addy asked, intrigued by this glimpse into the masculine mind.

"Them you keep where they'll do the least damage, and keep in mind always that they *are* the enemy. Trust them, but only so far. Keep them close, but not so close they can put a knife in you. And never tell them other than what you want them to carry back to your enemy's camp."

Because it made such sense, Addy offered no argument. But the viscount's observation made her even more aware of how very different he was from the other men she'd tutored. None of them possessed such cold intelligence and supreme self-confidence, and she wondered how much longer his lordship would stand in need of her services. Given the strides he had already made, he could doubtlessly take on a battalion of the ton's most imperious members, and emerge the victor. The thought was as unexpectedly disheartening as it was pleasing.

Aunt Matilda joined them, and they spent the afternoon reviewing everything the viscount would need to know to get through the evening. He'd mastered the necessary arrogance and charm required of his rank with equal success, but Addy decided his flirting skills needed a bit of work.

"There will be several eligible young ladies at tonight's ball," she told him as they took a break from training to enjoy a bit of luncheon. "You will want to have at least two of them falling at your feet by evening's end. No man is counted a complete success until he has set a few chits to swooning in the course of the Season."

To her amusement, an appalled look flashed across the viscount's face. "You're mad," he said, a faint tide of red washing over his tanned cheeks. "That's the most ridiculous thing I have ever heard! As if any man should want a female who behaved so foolishly!"

"Of course it's nonsense, lad; we are speaking of Society," Aunt Matilda counseled in her practical manner. "And as for your not wanting one of those tiresome chits, that's hardly the issue, is it? The issue is to make them want you. How else are we to get them to have their papas invite you to their homes?"

"I still think it's naught but foolishness," he grumbled, glaring at Addy as if suspecting her of trickery. "It cannot be true."

"Every word, my lord," she assured him solemnly. "And you needn't look so outraged. At least you're not the one expected to collapse like a souffle merely because some man has deigned to glance in your direction."

He set his wine glass down with a thump. "Are you

saying you have swooned at some man's feet?" he demanded.

Addy opened her lips to deny the charge, but her aunt answered for her.

"Adalaide?" she chortled, delicately covering her mouth with her napkin. *"Swoon?* If only she had done so! Then she might have managed to snare herself a husband, instead of going through three Seasons without receiving a single offer."

Even though it was nothing less than the truth, Addy flushed with mortification. "Stuff," she said, hiding her humiliation with a sniff. "One snares rabbits, Aunt, not husbands. Besides, even if I'd received a dozen offers, the result would have been the same. A spinster I am, and a spinster I mean to remain."

"You can see, my lord, the cross I am made to bear," Aunt Matilda mourned, turning to St. Jerome with a put-upon sigh. "Whatever am I to do with so unnatural a creature? I do not suppose you would consent to marry her?"

Addy's fork clattered to the table. "Aunt Matilda!"

"Oh, do not put yourself in such a taking, Adalaide," her aunt retorted, shaking her head. "His lordship knows quite well I was only funning. Don't you, my lord?"

"Indeed, Lady Fareham, I did not," the treacherous viscount responded, sounding absurdly downcast. "Does this mean my offer will not be considered?"

"Considered?" Aunt Matilda gave another cackle of laughter. "Dear boy, did I think you in earnest, I should have accepted before you had the words half out of your mouth!"

Addy managed a smile, even as her heart was twisting

in her chest. She was accustomed to being teased for her odd views on the married state, but for reasons she could not fathom, it hurt that his lordship should make a jest of marrying her. Perhaps Reginald was right and she'd grown rigid and humorless in her dotage, she thought. The prospect was nearly as displeasing as being a wife.

"Miss Terrington?" Lord St. Jerome reached out and covered her hand with his own. "Are you all right? 'Twas only a joke, you know. We meant no offense."

She was quick to gather her wits and her pride about her. "Who is offended?" she asked, feigning innocence. "I was planning my trousseau."

He jerked back his hand as if her flesh had become overheated. "Your trousseau?"

"Mmmm." She nibbled on a bite of salmon pie, pretending to linger over the delicate flavor. "There are many, sir, who would consider your words an offer in form. But don't worry," she added, smiling at his horrified expression, "I shan't hold you to them. Have you tried the fish? Cook is a wizard with sauce."

Six hours later Ross stood before his glass, staring at the reflection of a stranger.

"Is everything to your liking, my lord?" Joseph hovered at his elbow, wringing his hands in agitation. "I know the cravat is higher than you like, but it is all the rage, I do assure you. I—I can tie another, if you wish."

He sounded so near to tears at the prospect, Ross decided to take pity upon him. "No, Joseph, this will be fine, I thank you. 'Tis only that I am accustomed to seeing myself in uniform, and 'tis something of a shock to see myself rigged out in a gentleman's togs."

Joseph rose on tiptoe to run the brush over Ross's shoulders. "As if one should mention an ill-sewn Army jacket and one cut by Weston himself in the same breath," he said in accents of horror. "There is simply no comparison."

Ross merely shrugged. He'd left Miss Terrington's with precise instructions as to what he should wear, and it mattered riot to him how it looked. He glanced again at his reflection, thinking that if discomfort was any measure of style, then the jacket he was stuffed into had to be the most fashionable garment in the whole of London.

Cut from black velvet, with wide lapels and claw-hammer tails, the jacket clung tightly to his shoulders and arms. It was handsome enough, but it restricted his movements in a manner he found singularly distracting. How the devil was a man to draw a sword or fire a weapon trussed up like a roasting chicken?

Then there were the oyster-colored evening breeches Miss Terrington had insisted he wear. They were made of satin, and their indecent fit had him praying he would make it through the evening without splitting the seams. *That* would set the chits to swooning and make no doubt, he thought, his lips curving as he imagined the scandalous scene that would likely ensure. He wondered if his exacting instructress would be pleased or furious.

"His lordship left a rather extensive collection of jewels," Joseph said, offering Ross a flat velvet-colored case. "Perhaps you might find something to suit you."

Curious, Ross flicked open the case, and what he found nearly had the eyes popping out of his head.

"Good God!" he exclaimed, staring down at the glittering array in amazement. "There must be a fortune here!"

Nevil, who was now dressed in one of Ross's newer jackets and breeches, stepped forward to examine the box. "Looks like one of them treasure chests you hear about," he decided. "Your uncle must have been a regular peacock to be needing all of this."

"He might have needed it, but I do not," Ross replied, holding up a length of gold chain ending in a sparkling diamond fob and examining it with a glare. Satins and velvet were one thing, he decided, but his Scots practicality was outraged at the thought of such a foolish waste of money. "What the devil am I to do with it?"

"Wear 'em," Nevil advised, giving Ross a knowing look. "Let the enemy know you've the cannon to back your infantry. It will make them respect you, and that will make victory all the easier."

Because he could see the tactical sense of that, Ross slipped on the gold signet ring with his family's crest laid out in jewels. He also submitted to Joseph's suggestion of a stickpin topped with an emerald, but he coldly drew the line at wearing anything else. He was about to order the case put away when a flash of brilliant blue caught his eye.

"Wait, what is this?" he asked, and then the breath lodged in his throat when he lifted up a stunning necklace of icy diamonds and sapphires.

"Ah, that is the necklace Mr. McNeil spoke of," Joseph said, inching forward to gaze down at the necklace in awe. "Your uncle had it designed for the young lady he meant to marry, but the poor child died a few weeks before the wedding. His lordship never recovered, he said."

Ross stared at the necklace in silence, trying to think of the hard, hateful old man as a young man so in love that his fiancée's death left him bitter and broken. Or perhaps the marriage was but one of convenience, he decided, and his uncle had regarded the purchase of the necklace as nothing more than a shrewd investment. Certainly that would fit the image of the vindictive and controlling man Ross remembered. But as he studied the flash and dazzle of the exquisite jewels, he realized he had wronged his uncle. This was a gift of the heart. A gift of love that had become a painful and permanent reminder of what might have been. He returned the necklace to its velvet bed, thinking the blue stones were nearly the color of Miss Terrington's eyes.

"It's very lovely," he said quietly, closing the lid and handing the case back to Joseph. "And valuable as well. I wonder my cousin didn't take it with him when he left."

"Oh, he tried, my lord." Joseph smirked in satisfaction. "But your uncle's solicitors had anticipated such an action, and the jewels were kept in the solicitors' safe until it was certain you would be accepting the title. Mr. Atherton," he added with a prim sniff, "was said to be quite put out."

After his valet left, Ross ran a hand through his hair, disrupting the curls Joseph had taken such pains to arrange. "Bloody nonsense," he told Nevil, brushing the golden strands to his own satisfaction. "They might dress me like a useless dandy, but I'll be damned if they'll make me into one. They'll be after painting my face next, I'll warrant."

"No need to fear that, Sergeant." Nevil chuckled. "Joseph let slip how delighted he was that you was so tanned. No need to slap on the walnut stain, he said."

Ross repressed a shudder. During his recuperation he'd overheard Miss Terrington and her aunt debating whether or not they would have to resort to cosmetics to give him the proper appearance of manly vigor. Lady Fareham was against it, bless her, but Miss Terrington was of the opinion it might prove just the thing. It was all the rage amongst the Corinthians, apparently, and Ross remembered shaking his head at the foolishness of *Sassenachs*. If a man wanted a tanned complexion, why didn't he simply go out into the fields for a good day's work?

"I did as you asked," Nevil continued, comfortable with Ross's silence. "Only new man to hire on is George, one of the downstairs footmen. The others have been here since your uncle's time, and they've not but ill to speak of your cousin. A vicious, sorry sort he seems to have been, and I doubt any of them would so much as lift a finger to aid him."

"Keep an eye on George while he's in the house," Ross decided, realizing it was time to go. His stomach gave an uncomfortable lurch, but he sternly refused to call it fear. That would be too lowering to even consider.

"And when he's away from it, what then?" Nevil wanted to know. "If you wish, I've some comrades, former soldiers like myself, in need of honest employment. I could ask them to keep watch on him. Higgins would do best. He was one of Wellington's spies until a blasted infection took his leg."

"Hire him," Ross said at once. "Any man who can please the general will do well enough for me."

"What of the others?"

"Hire them as well," Ross told him, realizing with a jolt the good he could now do as a wealthy man. "In fact, spread the word amongst your friends. Any former soldier in need of employ is to come to me. I will see he is given work."

Nevil studied him thoughtfully. "I know what you're about, Sergeant," he said in a gentle voice, "and I think the better of you for it. But there are thousands in need of assistance in London alone. You cannot help them all."

"No," Ross agreed, accepting the bitter truth of the corporal's words. "But I will help all that I am able. I may not have wanted this cursed title and the money that came with it, but 'tis mine now, and I will do with it what I wish."

"You sound rather certain of that," Nevil observed shrewdly. "Reached a decision, have you?"

Ross paused, his hand on the door. "Yes," he said slowly. "I have. By God, I have. Good evening to you, Corporal Collier." And with that he turned and left the room.

The carriage was waiting for him, and he was soon on his way to meet Miss Terrington and her aunt. On the short journey to Bruton Street he sat back against the plush squabs and ruthlessly laid out a new plan of attack. Miss Terrington had given him the weapons he needed for the coming battle, and for that he was grateful, but 'twas time he took command of the operation. His little general mightn't know it as yet, but the troops had just mutinied. It would be interesting to see how she accepted the news.

Five

"Adalaide, if you don't cease that wretched pacing and sit down, I vow I shall have you lashed to your chair!"

Lady Fareham stood in the center of the drawing room, her arms folded across her chest and a look of severest censure upon her face. It was an expression Addy had seen many times, but she was too distracted to do other than shoot her aunt an apologetic look.

"I'm sorry, Aunt," she said, even as she kept moving restlessly about the room. "But I am so nervous, I couldn't stay still did my life depend upon it."

"If you don't stop hopping about like a flea, it well could," the older woman retorted with a dark mutter. "The way you're going on, one would think 'twas you about to make your bows rather than his lordship. Sit down, child."

When her aunt used that tone, Addy knew better than to disobey. She lowered herself onto the nearest chair, her fingers drumming out an impatient tattoo. "It's too soon," she said, her mind racing as she considered all that lay ahead of them. "We're rushing our fences. The viscount isn't ready for this. We've had scarce a sennight to bring him up to scratch, and that's not nearly enough time." She leapt to her feet. "I'll send a note to Lord Creshton offering our regrets. I'm sure he—"

"Adalaide Margurite, I said *sit down!*"

Startled, Addy complied with an unladylike *plop.* "I'm sorry," she repeated, genuinely contrite. "But you must see how very unfair we are being to Lord St. Jerome! All my other pupils have had their entire lives to come to terms with their stations, but his lordship hasn't even had a month, and he was ill for most of that!"

Aunt Matilda studied her for several seconds before responding. "Are you saying he is not capable of carrying out his task?" she demanded bluntly.

"Of course not!" Addy rallied to the viscount's defense like a mama bear protecting her cub. "His lordship is quite the most intelligent of all my pupils! I have never had any gentleman take to instruction half so quickly."

"Then why are you in such a bother?"

"I—" Addy started to answer, and then stopped. "I don't know," she admitted, staring at her aunt. "It's not the viscount's abilities I mistrust so much as I mistrust—"

"So much as you mistrust your own," Aunt Matilda finished with a sympathetic nod. "I understand. The task you've undertaken is daunting enough to give a saint pause, but you've done as well as you could."

"Come, child," she added as Addy opened her lips in protest, "be honest. Would he be any more ready than he is now if you had another week to prepare? Another day?"

Addy thought of the cool, confident man who'd taken his leave of them a few hours earlier, and compared him to some of the men she'd spent months preparing for just such a night. "No," she said softly, grateful for her aunt's cool practicality. "No, Aunt, he would not."

"Good." Her aunt gave a decisive nod. "Now that that is behind us, tell me your plans for the evening."

Addy reviewed her meticulously timed schedule. "I thought I would rendezvous with Lord Creshton and the others to see if there have been any new developments in Parliament," she said thoughtfully. "Then I was going to speak with the men his grace has picked to put his lordship up for membership in the clubs. Oh, and I must have a word with Lady Kirkson about her daughters. They are both the acclaimed beauties of the Season, and if we could get one of them to—"

"I didn't mean your plans for St. Jerome," Aunt Matilda interrupted, scowling. "I meant your plans for yourself."

Addy stared at her in confusion. "Those are my plans for myself."

Her aunt raised her eyes heavenward. "Good Lord preserve me, the girl is as thick as a plank."

"Aunt Matilda, what are you talking about?"

"I am talking, young lady, about the fact you are going to be spending the better part of the evening in the company of some of the most eligible men in the country. This is an opportunity any female with half a brain in her head dreams of, and I want to know what you intend doing about it!"

Understanding dawned, and Addy shook her head in gentle rebuke. "Aunt, how many times must I remind you I am no longer on the catch for a husband? I've put on my caps, for heaven's sake!" She indicated the prim twist of gray sarcenet ruthlessly covering her copper-colored curls.

Her aunt gave a sniff of patent disapproval. "Pray don't remind me of that," she said. "A bigger scandal than a girl scarce out of her teens donning a widow's weeds and acting like a dowager, I've yet to see. I quite wonder the Patronesses allow you such conceit."

"Perhaps because they appreciate my willingness to accept the unvarnished truth," Addy replied calmly. "Aunt Matilda, we have had this discussion *ad nauseum,* and you know I have the right of it. If I am to continue helping others as I have helped his lordship, then I must make it plain I am not doing so merely to trap some poor gentleman into marriage. The only way I can do that and keep any pretense of pride is to pin up my hair and declare myself a spinster before someone else can do it for me."

"I realize that," her aunt conceded with a disgruntled glare, "but that doesn't mean you risk the scandal of the Season merely by dancing. And if you're so determined to help St. Jerome, hasn't it occurred to you that you'll do him far more good on the dance floor than if you spend the entire evening stuffed away in some corner?"

Addy sat back in her chair. "That is so," she said, impressed with her aunt's canny reasoning. "Very well, ma'am, should a gentleman ask for a dance I promise to consider the matter before saying no. Is that agreeable?"

"No, but I'm not such a fool as to think I shall do

better," Aunt Matilda retorted. "Ah, well, one can only hope the prime minister will deign to stand up with you. Perhaps you're not so toplofty as to turn down a peer."

She and Addy continued chatting until Lord St. Jerome came striding into the room. Addy glanced up, the words of greeting she'd been about to utter withering on her lips. The viscount noted her wide-eyed stare and came to an uncertain halt.

"What is it?" he demanded, reaching for the intricate cravat knotted beneath his chin. "Is it this cursed thing? My valet insisted 'twas all the fashion."

It took a moment before Addy was able to find her voice. "And so it is," she said, gathering her composure with an effort. "Pray accept my apologies for staring, my lord. I fear I was lost in thought. But you are looking quite nice, I must say. Your valet is to be complimented."

"Quite nice?" her aunt echoed, gaping at her as if she was bereft of reason. "Has your eyesight gone begging along with your wits? The lad is an Adonis!" She turned back to St. Jerome, who was red-faced with embarrassment.

"You are looking as fine as a sixpence, my boy," she said, thrusting out her gloved hand and beaming up at him in approval. "There'll not be a feminine heart safe this night, I'll be bound."

Addy could think of nothing more to say, and to cover her discomfit she gathered up her shawl and fan. "If you are ready, my lord, we had best be on our way," she said, rising gracefully to her feet. "As you are the guest of honor, it would hardly do for us to be late."

The viscount raised his eyebrows at her clipped tone, but to her relief he offered her no comment. A short while later they were on their way, and while her aunt and St. Jerome chatted, Addy took the opportunity to study his lordship without fear of being observed.

The black velvet jacket, silver and cream satin waistcoat, and cream-colored breeches he was wearing were identical in every aspect to attire she'd seen on a hundred different men, but when he'd first walked into the drawing room she'd felt her heart stumble to a halt. She'd been aware of him as she'd never been aware of another man, and her unexpected and decidedly missish behavior left her both bewildered and ashamed.

The only explanation she could devise for such a sad want of conduct was that his lordship was an unusually handsome man. Her protestations to her aunt aside, she was still a female, and no more immune to masculine attractions than any other female. Indeed, she assured herself, it would have boded ill for their plans for the viscount had she *not* found him attractive. Given that it was natural she should be affected by his appearance, and now that she knew how devastating he could be in evening dress, she would be better prepared for the next time she saw him. It was all perfectly logical.

". . . do you not agree, Adalaide?" Her aunt was glancing at her expectantly.

Addy shifted uneasily, not trusting her aunt enough to agree to anything without knowing precisely what it was she was agreeing to. "Once again, I must apologize," she said, pleased with her cool tones. "I was thinking of something else, and fear I wasn't attending. What was it you were saying, Aunt?"

"Nothing of interest, 'twould seem," her aunt grumbled sourly. "Well, what was it you were thinking?

Something wicked, I've no doubt, if that cat-in-the-cream smirk of yours was any indication."

Addy felt her cheeks with consternation. "Not at all, my lady," she said, thinking her aunt must truly be the witch her brother Arthur sometimes called her. "I was thinking of tonight, and how we will go on."

"And what decisions have you reached, if I may ask?" Lord St. Jerome's genial tones made it plain he had decided to take pity on her.

"I've decided that since it's likely everyone in Society will have learned of your recent elevation to the peerage, we'd do better to utilize their curiosity rather than ignoring it," she said, thinking quickly. "They'll be expecting you to be overwhelmed by your new circumstances, and anxious as a puppy to make yourself agreeable."

"Aye," he agreed, inclining his head coolly. "So you have said. You have also said I should not oblige them, or have you changed your mind about that?"

"Indeed not!" she hurried to assure him. "As I've remarked, the *ton* dotes most on that which they consider just beyond their reach, and the more standoffish you are, the more ardently they shall pursue you."

"Yes, Miss Terrington," he replied in the manner of a young boy responding to an officious governess.

Feeling generous, Addy decided to ignore the provocation. "As the duke's guest of honor you'll be seated to his wife's right," she continued, going over ground they'd covered earlier that day. "Her grace is exceedingly fond of handsome young men, so you may count upon her to flirt with you. You're not to notice if she should pat your knee."

He looked momentarily alarmed. "Yes, Miss Terrington."

Addy shot him a suspicious look, but when he responded with a bland look of polite inquiry, she continued. "You may dance, if you wish, but mind to whom you make your bows. You must appear to be as selective as possible. The fewer times you stand up with the ladies, the greater an honor they shall deem it when you do ask them. You may look to Lord Falconer for direction in this matter. He almost never dances, and when he does, the young lady he singles out is instantly accounted a diamond of the first water."

"Yes, Miss Terrington."

She glared at him. "Can you say nothing other than 'Yes, Miss Terrington'?" she demanded crossly.

He studied her for several seconds, and then his lips curved in a smile that set her treacherous heart to thumping once more. "Yes, Miss Terrington."

"I'll say this for you, lad, you're a cool one under fire," the Duke of Creshton said, hiding a smile as the elderly woman stalked away, her face set in lines of extreme displeasure. "If Lady Percyville had interrogated me like that, I should have bolted for the border!"

Ross sent the woman a look tinged as much with respect as with resentment. "I was tempted, your grace, believe me," he said, thinking the old harridan could give lessons to the Intelligence Corps on how to question prisoners.

The duke gave a chuckle, clapping Ross companionably on the shoulder. "Well, our duty's done, Sergeant, and it's time to make merry. We've earned our right to a drop, I'd say."

Ross followed silently, the thought of a drink sorely tempting. He'd spent the better part of an hour being quizzed by an avid Society determined on ferreting out his every secret, and his temper was near to exploding. Only the knowledge he dared not risk the mission kept a civil tongue in his head, but even then he'd come perilously close to telling some impertinent *sassennach* precisely what he thought of them. 'Twas odd, he thought, as he and the duke made their way to the corner of the ballroom where liveried servants stood beside a table groaning under the weight of various delicacies. But the hotter the anger in his heart burned, the colder his expression grew, and the colder his expression, the more the English fawned upon him. Miss Terrington had the right of it, he decided, shaking his head in silent wonder. The *ton* were as mad as their king.

The duke handed Ross a glass of champagne and then lifted his own glass in toast. "Here's to you, my lord," he said, his weathered face wreathed in smiles. "You've done well for a first engagement. Wellington couldn't have hoped for a better champion!"

"Thank you, sir," Ross responded, pleased by the praise. "But 'tis Miss Terrington you ought to be congratulating. She has far more to do with this than do I."

"Quite so, young man, quite so," the duke agreed, giving another chuckle. "The lass is nearly as intimidating as Lady Percyville, and far lovelier. Where is the dear lady that I might tender her my thanks? Miss Terrington, that is, not Lady Percyville. Can't abide her above half a minute's time, don't you know."

Ross didn't need to look to know where to find his instructress. Even while bowing and scraping to the guests lined up to goggle at him, he'd been careful to keep his eye on Miss Terrington. He'd been amused to note her eye was on him as well, and the realization had filled him with an odd sense of contentment.

"She is over by the window, your grace, flirting with Lord Falconer."

The duke turned to peer in the direction Ross had indicated. "Is she, by gad? Ah, yes, I see them now. He's a fine man, I must say, and a good one, even if he's a trifle high in the instep. Hoped he and my elder daughter might make a match of it, but Elinore proclaimed him as cold and emotionless as a block of stone, and he named her a shrew of the first water." He glanced back at Ross, a speculative note gleaming in his eye.

"Don't suppose you'd be interested in marrying her?" he asked, sounding hopeful. "She's well dowered and well bred, for all she has a tongue like a cat-o'-nine-tails and a temper to match. She'd make you an excellent viscountess."

Ross couldn't say which shocked him more, that the duke would casually trot out his daughter's failings to a stranger, or that he would in the next breath offer her to that stranger with no more hesitation than if she was a horse he was offering for trade.

"That is very good of you, sir," he said hastily, thinking that for all the instruction Miss Terrington had taken such pains to give him, she hadn't told him how to handle so mortifying a situation. "But as I've yet to have the honor of making your daughter's acquaintance, I fear I cannot say. But I thank you for the honor," he added, hoping to avoid insulting the man who'd been so good to him.

"And you're not likely to meet her, considering the stubborn chit has buried herself in the country and won't come to London for love nor money," the duke muttered, shaking his head. "I married off both my heirs and my youngest daughter without an ounce of effort, but Elinore . . ." He shook his head a second time, his scowl melting into a smile of paternal indulgence. "The lass is me all over, may God help the poor man she sets her sights upon."

Ross was spared the necessity of reply by the arrival of Miss Terrington and Lord Falconer. She was smiling, and behind the lenses of her spectacles, her eyes were dancing sapphire-bright.

"Congratulations, my lord," she said, surprising him by dropping into a graceful curtsy. "You are an unqualified success. The ladies all think you utterly charming, and the men account you 'a good sort,' which is a compliment of the first order, or so I am told." She glanced at the marquess, who gave a cool nod of assent.

"Creighville and Longhead have spoken of putting you up for membership at White's," he said. "And Marchton is having your name put forward at Brook's."

"Only Marchton?" the duke demanded, looking displeased.

In answer Falconer's lips curved in a wolfish smile. "When 'tis Marchton, no other is needed," he said wryly. "A million pounds will do that for a man, to say nothing of the title he is said to have recently purchased."

Ross thought of the tanned and aloof man he'd been presented to earlier. No title and therefore no seat in the House of Lords to be courted, but the duke had treated him with a wary respect that had made Ross take note at once. He frowned as he recalled something the duke had told him.

"But he's an American," Ross said, recalling the way the man had gripped his hand with surprising strength.

"Of English descent," Falconer corrected. "His father was rumored to be an illegitimate son who went to the New World to seek his fortune about the time of the last war." He smiled again. "It would seem he found it."

"Speaking of Mr. Marchton"—Miss Terrington turned to Ross—"he'll be accompanying you and Lord Hixworth when you go to Tattersall's. He's anxious to buy breeding stock for his farm in Virginia, and the earl has promised to help."

The talk turned general, and the knot of tension coiling inside Ross slowly began unwinding. He found he could smile, even laugh, as they reviewed the night's successes and failures. To his relief, there were more of the former than the latter, and he was feeling cautiously optimistic as the tune the musicians were scratching out reached his ears. Recognizing one of the dances he'd so recently learned, he turned to Miss Terrington, a smile on his lips as he made an elaborate bow over her hand.

"If you've not pledged this dance to another, I should be honored if you would stand up with me," he said, amused to see both consternation and alarm on her pixielike face. 'Twas a rare thing for him to get the upper hand with the little *briosag,* and he meant to savor it while he could.

"Don't be absurd," she said, snatching back her hand and scowling up at him. "Don't you recall what I said about minding with whom you dance? If you're seen standing up with me, you'll be laughed out of London inside of an hour!"

He regained possession of her hand. "And are you so free with your favors, then, that you dance with every man jack who asks you?" he drawled, knowing well the answer.

"Of course not!" she exclaimed, clearly indignant at such a charge. "I never dance."

"Then what could better establish my reputation than to be seen dancing with a lady known for being particular in her choice of partners?" he asked, drawing her hand through his arm and turning toward the dance floor. "You said it yourself, ma'am. The choosier one is seen to be, the greater the honor for the one chosen. This way, if you please."

Amused at her muttering and the way she dragged her heels, he led her out on to the dance floor, where a set was forming. The music was light, the steps easy, and Ross gave himself up to the sheer joy of the music. He couldn't recall the last time he'd danced at a ball, nor even the last time he'd felt so lighthearted and carefree. Years of death and danger had taught him to treasure such moments, and when the dance ended he was beaming down at his partner.

"Would it risk my reputation and yours if we were to dance again?" he asked, taking in her appearance in delight. Her spectacles were askew, her cheeks prettily flushed, and more than a few flame-colored tendrils had escaped confinement to riot about her forehead and dainty ears. He thought he'd never seen a sight more charming.

"It most certainly would," she retorted, straightening her spectacles with a glare. "Now take yourself off to some corner to look down at the rest of us in lordly arrogance before you undo all the good we've accomplished." And with that she trounced off, her own nose held at a suitably arrogant angle that had Ross chuckling in amusement.

Hoist with her own petard. The phrase flashed through Addy's mind as she ducked behind the potted palm standing forlornly in the corner of the ballroom. She'd only just succeeded in shedding her last partner, and she was determined to remain hidden until her current partner gave up searching for her and wandered off to find some other poor female to pester. It was her fault, she supposed, and knowing she was to blame for her present difficulties did little to soothe her sensibilities.

Her observation that dancing with Lord St. Jerome would make a lady the belle of the ball had proven all too prophetic. The dance with his lordship had scarce ended before she found herself besieged by eager men, all begging her for a dance. Her initial response was to refuse, but with her aunt's admonishment in mind, she'd grudgingly changed her mind. Instead of retreating, she'd stood up with two or three gentlemen she thought might help further St. Jerome's cause. Once she'd done that, the race was on.

It had been years since she'd danced with someone other than one of her pupils or some long-suffering friend of her brothers. Having a man actually *want* to dance with her had proven an interesting novelty, and one she was honest enough to admit she enjoyed. That was why she had danced more than she ought to have done. But when she realized the other guests were watching her and whispering behind their hands, sanity had prevailed, and she'd decided enough was enough.

The autocratic dowagers who ruled Society might be willing to overlook an on-the-shelf spinster engaging in an occasional bout of dancing, but did she appear to make a habit of it, they could well change their minds. It had taken her years to convince the old biddies she had no interest in attracting a husband, and if she began dancing again, they could begin questioning her sincerity. She could even find herself being regarded as an eligible female, and that would put paid to all of her carefully laid plans.

"Your pardon, Miss Terrington, but are you hiding from an ambush, or preparing for one?"

The low, masculine drawl had Addy jolting in alarm, and she spun around to find herself gazing up into the sardonic face of the viscount. Operating on the principle that 'twas better to attack than to defend, she rose to her full height and fixed him with her frostiest look.

"I beg your pardon, my lord," she said, adopting her most imperious demeanor. "But I am sure I have no notion what you might be referring to."

"If 'tis an ambush you're seeking to avoid," he continued, acting for all the world as if she hadn't spoken, "I should be more than happy to provide cover. But if 'tis an ambush you were meaning to spring, I take leave to tell you you have already committed a tactical error."

Dimples flashed in his lean cheeks. "Your flank was exposed."

"Oh!" Addy's cheeks fired with indignation. The remark skated the edge of what was acceptable; a fact she was quick to point out to his lordship.

"Gentlemen do not speak of such things to young ladies," she told him tartly. "Mind you don't do so again."

"As you say," he agreed. "And now that you've done dressing me down, tell me why you have gone into hiding." The emerald-green of his eyes grew hard. "Has some man offered you insult? If so, you must point him out to me that I might have words with him. I'll not have you treated so poorly by the likes of them."

He sounded so dangerous, so untamed, Addy took a step closer. "Of course not," she assured him, laying a restraining hand on his arm. Then, lest he take her for some silly milk-and-water miss, she added, "But if one had, *I* should be the one to deal with him. Is that understood?"

He stared down at her for a long moment before his lips lifted in a reluctant smile. "Aye," he said at last, and then shocked her by lifting a hand to gently touch her cheek. "You're a fierce one, to be sure, but for all of that you're still a woman. Any man who harms or insults you will pay dearly for it."

Addy hadn't the words for the emotions rioting through her. On one level, she was indignant he should think she either wanted or needed his protection, but on another level, she felt a thrill of relief to know someone cared. That he cared. She moved away, turning from her own weakness as much as from him.

"If you'll excuse me, my lord, I was about to take a breath of fresh air," she said, striving for her usual sense of cool command. "It is rather close in here, and I am beginning to feel unwell."

She knew from the flare of awareness in his eyes that he didn't believe her. A gentleman would have taken the hint and departed, but her pupil was no gentleman.

"If you're unwell, then I shall be pleased to act as your escort," he said, stepping toward her with obvious purpose.

Knowing a struggle would bring unwanted attention down upon them, Addy could only glare at him. But she still had her pride, and it was she who led the way out onto the small stone balcony located just off the crowded ballroom.

The night was misty and cool, the brisk air washing over her heated cheeks with the softest of touches. The French doors were standing slightly open, and the murmur of music and voices flowed out into the night. Addy stood in silence, her chilled arms wrapped lightly about her. She would remain here for a few more minutes, she decided, and then they would go back inside. But one minute slid easily into another, and still Addy remained where she was; loath to leave the coolness and the peace she had found.

"Are you feeling better?" The viscount was standing beside her, studying her in the soft light streaming through the doors.

"Yes," Addy said, turning to him with a half smile. "You do know I was trying to be rid of you?" she asked ruefully, her anger having long since faded.

His grin flashed. "A bit thickheaded I may be, but not

so thickheaded as that," he said, chuckling. "And a word of warning to you, Miss Terrington, if I might. If you're truly intent upon having a man gone, never let him suspect it. A man has his pride, you know, and we can none of us resist a challenge."

Addy considered that, and then nodded. "I suppose not," she agreed, thinking what perverse creatures men were. "But it seems highly unfair to me. What is a female to do? If we ask you to stay, we are a flirt, if we tell you to go, we are a challenge." She sighed again, and then slid a thoughtful glance at the viscount's moonlit countenance. "How are you?" she asked softly. "Is it going well?"

To her relief, he took her meaning at once. "Aye," he said, leaning against the stone balustrade and staring out into the darkness. "The general has many friends, and they are all of them eager to help. But he has his enemies as well. I was interested to see that his lordship has both in equal number here tonight."

Addy smiled at the observation. "That was the idea," she reminded him. "How can you be expected to change their minds if you don't meet them?"

He gave a soft laugh. "That's sensible, then."

"And did you?" she asked curiously.

"Did I what?"

"Did you change any minds?"

He was a moment in answering. "Perhaps. The Earl of Carnforth seemed interested enough when I spoke with him. He asked a dozen questions, but listened closely to the answers I gave. He asked me to join him at his country house for some weekend, and I said that I would." He sent her a sharp glance. "Is that all right?"

"Certainly," she assured him, pleased at how well it was all going. "Who else did you speak with?"

He dutifully rattled off a list that had Addy beaming. For a start it was most impressive, and they spent the next quarter-hour discussing how best to proceed. She was about to suggest they return to the ballroom when he suddenly paused, his head titled to one side as he listened to the soft music flowing into the night.

"What song is that they are playing?" he asked curiously. " 'Tis lovely."

Addy listened to the delicate sounds of violin and pianoforte blending together in absolute harmony. "I'm not certain," she admitted, feeling slightly apologetic. "I fear I'm not at all musical, but I believe it's a quadrille."

They listened for a few more notes, and then he turned to her, his hands held out in silent command. "Dance with me," he ordered softly.

Addy gaped at him, appalled at the way her pulse was racing wildly out of control at the very thought. "Dance with you?" she echoed, struggling to gather her scattered thoughts into some semblance of order. "Don't be absurd, sir," she scoffed, her voice sounded breathless and too soft even to her ears. "It would be most improper to do so."

"Who is to see?" he asked, his hand steady as his gaze met hers. "Dance with me, Adalaide. Please."

Whether it was the sound of her name or the soft plea in his voice, Addy could not say. She found herself moving forward, her fingers curling around his as he drew her against him. Their palms touched, and then with only the moon to witness, they circled about each other in time to the lilting music.

Six

The next fortnight flew past for Ross. The ball at the duke's home was but the first in a dizzying whirl of such frivolous activities, and each night found him at some foolish ball or fete. He hated the endless bowing and scraping, the way people who normally would have turned their noses up at him now fell over their well-shod feet to gain his approval. Not because of who he was, he thought bitterly, but rather because of what he was. A viscount, and a man rich enough to have the matchmaking mamas rubbing their hands together in greedy glee.

But disgusted as he was, even he had to admit the situation was not without its benefits. With Nevil's assistance he was able to help several cashiered soldiers find employment, and others he aided with money and a kind word. It was little enough, but it was something, and he felt better for being of some good to the men. He also took a grim satisfaction in knowing how his uncle would have howled to see his gold put to such use.

He'd made friends as well. Despite the disparity in the ages and situations, he and Lord Hixworth had become fast friends, and he admired the younger man for his horse sense and kind heart. Both Lord Falconer and the Earl of Denbury became frequent visitors at his house, and he at theirs. He'd never thought to be at such ease with men of rank and wealth, and yet somehow he was. Denbury was loquacious and bright as sunshine, Falconer cool and distant as a storm in the mountains, and yet Ross trusted and liked them both.

At the moment they were in his study, enjoying a comfortable glass of the Spanish brandy the earl had brought with him. They'd spent the day going over the news from Spain, and debating when and how to use the information.

"The victories are small, but frequent enough to show Wellington's plans are working," Falconer said, leaning back in his chair and looking thoughtful. "A decisive victory is what's needed; one convincing enough to silence his critics for all time."

Ross remained silent. He agreed with Falconer's assessment, but as a soldier he knew the price such a victory would demand. The dead piled upon the dead, like at Badajoz, a scene so horrific it was burned deep into his very soul. "We have the French on the run," he said, the brandy burning his throat as he took a deep sip. "With the mountains in front of them and the British Army in back of them, they'll have no choice but to make a stand. When they do you'll have your victory, my lords, I promise you."

"Where do you think the stand will occur?"

Ross's gaze flicked to the map of Spain spread out on the table. "Here," he said, indicating a narrow gap in the mountains. "The French will gather there to prepare for their retreat. They'll need to mount a rear-guard action to cover them, and that's where they'll fight."

"When?" This from Denbury, who was leaning forward and looking as grim as Ross felt.

Did they think him a *faidhean,* then, to know the future? Ross wondered, thrusting an impatient hand through his hair. He rose to his feet and prowled over to stand before the window. May was half gone, and the wee garden was in gentle bloom. In Spain the heat would be building, and the soldiers would be suffering from the sun as they'd suffered from the wind and the cold. The French would be suffering too, and this time they would be the ones in full flight.

"Soon," he said at last, turning back to face the others. "With each day we grow greater in numbers and better armed. Napoleon is too wise a campaigner to let us grow too strong, and I'm guessing he'll order Jourdan to turn and attack."

"Then if we can hold off a call for a vote, we could win," Falconer said, stroking a finger across his chin. "That shouldn't be too difficult. We've only to open up the matter for another debate, and they'll talk themselves hoarse until summer's come and gone."

"Speaking of debates, my lord, your maiden speech is set for next week," the earl reminded Ross. "How is it coming? I should be happy to help you with it, if need be. I've always had a way with words."

"Too much of a way," Falconer retorted, the gleam in his eyes softening the criticism. "We don't want St. Jerome boring our foes into submission."

"So long as do they submit, what does it matter?"

Denbury asked with a shrug. "But my offer stands, Sergeant. You've but to say the word."

Ross sent him a grateful look. "Thank you, my lord," he said, meaning every word. "I may well take you up on your offer. For all of her instructions, Miss Terrington has yet to teach me the proper way to stand and address Parliament."

"Give her time, old fellow," Denbury said with a warm chuckle. "She will. Remember Letham?" he asked in an aside to Falconer. "Lad couldn't string two words together without swooning before The Terror got her hands on him. Now he can jaw with the best of them."

"The Terror?" Ross echoed, wondering if he'd hear aright.

"Miss Terrington," Denbury elaborated. "It's what she's called, don't you see. 'The Terror of the Terringtons.' And one must say the name is rather fitting. Heaven only knows she terrifies me." And he laughed as if he thought it the merriest joke he had ever heard.

Ross's contentment was swamped by a wave of icy fury. Even knowing the earl was jesting did little to ease his anger, and it was a moment before he could speak.

"I do not believe I care to have Miss Terrington addressed in so slighting a manner," he said, his voice harsh. "You will oblige me by not doing so again."

For all he was as affable a man as Ross had ever met, Denbury was no one's fool. He studied Ross for several seconds before slowly inclining his head. "As you wish, my lord," he replied, his tone matching Ross's for coolness. "I beg pardon if I have given offense."

Ross felt an uncomfortable prick of remorse at the earl's stilted apology. "Now 'tis I who am obliged to beg your pardon," he said, offering the other man a rueful smile. "I'm not offended, Denbury, I'm . . . nervous, I suppose you would say," he admitted, seizing on the first emotion he could find. "I've fought my way out of ambushes outnumbered three to one and not been half so terrified. The thought of speaking in front of others has me quaking like a virgin facing her first man."

"An interesting comparison, St. Jerome," Falconer observed with a low drawl. "Would you not say so, Denbury?"

"And an accurate one." Denbury's easy grin made it plain he bore Ross no ill will. "Politics is near as complicated as lovemaking, and not nearly so pleasurable. But never fear, sir. You mastered the one, you'll master the other."

The talk turned general, and a short while later Denbury took his leave. Ross wasn't surprised when Falconer chose to remain behind. The viscount had had his ears pinned back too many times not to recognize the determined set of the marquess's jaw, and the moment they were alone he turned to face him.

"Before you say another word, sir, I know I was in the wrong," Ross said, standing rigidly at attention. "Lord Denbury was but making an observation, and I had no right to take his nose off for him."

Falconer remained silent, his expression enigmatic as he studied Ross. "Indeed?" he said quietly. "It is good of you to tell me so, for I was about to apologize for Denbury. I am glad to have been spared the effort."

"*You* were about to apologize to *me?*" Ross's tone was incredulous. "Good God, why?"

"Because for all she has a viper's tongue and a

shrew's disposition, Miss Terrington is a very admirable female, and one I do not care to be slighted."

The simple explanation left Ross feeling even more confused, and he collapsed on his chair with an angry scowl. "Then why the devil didn't you say so?" he demanded indignantly. " 'Twould have sounded better coming from you than from me."

"Why should that be?" Falconer asked. "You're better acquainted with the lady than am I. You are her natural champion. Who better to defend her?"

Ross wasn't certain what to make of that. "You're an odd one, my lord," he said, leaning back his head and studying the marquess with narrowed eyes. "Sometimes I wonder what there is to you."

Falconer's lips curved in a cool smile. "Perhaps that is the way I prefer it."

"And perhaps that says more about you than you may know," Ross said. "I will tell you this much, 'tis glad I am to have you standing with me, rather than against me. You would make a deadly opponent."

Falconer's gold-colored eyes flared with pleasure. "You do me credit, sir. Coming from a warrior such as yourself, that is a compliment of the first order. I will return it by saying I am equally relieved to have you with us. And you would honor me by calling me by my given name. 'Tis Adam," he added at Ross's blank look.

"And I am Ross," Ross said, smiling. "Now that that is done, is there anything else you would care to discuss? I've another blasted ball to attend tonight, and my valet will be after me to be getting ready."

"Valets are the cross we gentlemen must bear," Adam

agreed. "Mine is a terror. But there is something I would discuss with you. It concerns Miss Terrington."

Ross tensed as if for a blow. "What is it?"

"Your lessons, do they continue?"

"Some," Ross replied, wondering what Adam was about. "I spend an hour or so each day with her and Lady Fareham, and there are usually lessons to be had. Yesterday she wanted Hixworth and me to practice with quizzing glasses," he added, his brow darkening in indignation, "but I told her I'd be cursed before I would resort to such dandified nonsense."

"And knowing Miss Terrington, I daresay she said she would be cursed if you did not," Adam said, then laughed at Ross's mutinous expression. "Don't look so black, my lord. It's not so bad as all that. Even I have been known to resort to such theatrics, and I've not the advantage of Miss Terrington's instruction."

"She told me later it was more for Hixworth's benefit than my own," he grumbled, smiling at the memory of the way she'd glowered at him like a furious sprite. "She said he needs it for confidence, and that it would do me no harm to use it as well."

"It sounds like her," Adam said, chuckling. "But the reason I mention lessons is because I think it would be best if you discontinue with them; for the moment, at least."

Ross jerked his head back in surprise. He could not explain why, but for some reason the notion of not seeing Adalaide—Miss Terrington, he corrected himself— was oddly troubling. She'd been the first person he'd come to know in his new life. She was a constant, always there to hector and peck at him. Not to see her for days on end . . .

"May I ask why?" he demanded, suspicion having his hands clenching into angry fists. "If someone's dared to speak a word against her, I'll cut the tongues from their heads."

"An admirable if slightly gruesome sentiment," Falconer agreed, "but as it happens, there isn't any talk. Or at least," he added, "not any more than should be expected. This is the Marriage Mart, after all, and matches are an endless source of speculation and entertainment for us all."

"Then why should I avoid Miss Terrington?"

"I haven't said you should avoid her," Adam said carefully. "It's merely that it would be best for all concerned if the lessons were to be temporarily suspended. Once it's seen you're a gentleman in your own right and not some male version of Pygmalion, the tattle will die down—"

Ross was on his feet in a flash, his eyes bright with fury as he faced Falconer. "I thought you said there was no talk about Adalaide!" he said, her Christian name slipping from his lips in his distress.

"There's not," Falconer responded, rising cautiously to his feet. "The talk is all of you."

"Me?" Ross was stunned.

"Aye," the marquess said coolly. "You. It is being put about that when you arrived in London you were one step removed from a barbarian. Filthy, half-wild, and the farthest thing from a gentleman that one may imagine. Miss Terrington is well known for her ability to work miracles, and it is said she has worked her biggest one with you."

Ross's pride took the blow, and he shrugged it off. "Well, 'tis true enough when you think of it," he said, remembering the way he'd collapsed on Adalaide's doorstep. "Let them say what they will. I care not."

"But we must care," Adam corrected with a cool look. "Your sudden appearance is the object of a great deal of speculation. We knew it would be, and we'd planned to use that speculation to our own advantage. The *ton* is like a bored child forever in search of a new toy to amuse them—"

"And you thought to make me that toy," Ross finished, his lips thinning in anger. "Why are you so distressed, then? 'Twould seem you have your wish."

"Some speculation is acceptable, even desired, but we cannot have it put about that you are little more than a marionette whose strings are being pulled for him."

Ross's pride took another, more painful blow as he faced a bitter truth. "Even if that is what I am?"

"Especially if that is what you are," Adam said bluntly, his expression remorseless. "I do not say these things to cause you hurt, or to make you feel I think less of you. I say them because they are necessary. Society may wonder about you all they please, and it is all for the good. But if they laugh at you, if they dismiss you as little more than a country bumpkin, then you are worse than useless to us. You are a hindrance."

Resentment and fury threatened, but Ross kept them in icy check. " 'Tis as well you mean me no harm, Falconer," he said with a harsh laugh. "Else I would surely be a dead man. Very well, my lord, no more lessons, then."

If Falconer noticed Ross's use of his title, he gave no indication. "You will need to attend more balls and the like," he continued in his matter-of-fact manner. "The more you are seen about town, the sooner these tiresome rumors will fade. In the meanwhile, I've arranged for you to be admitted to Almack's. Your first presentation will be this Wednesday. It's a bit late in the Season so it won't be a formal presentation, but it will be enough to show you are accepted at the highest levels."

Adalaide had also spoken of getting him admitted to Almack's, Ross remembered, her bright blue eyes dancing with excitement as she'd plotted how to get him one of the coveted vouchers. She and her aunt had gone over a list of people they could browbeat into helping them, and he'd leaned back in his chair doing his best not to grin.

"St. Jerome?" Falconer's voice was sharp, recalling Ross to the present. He stirred slightly, meeting the other man's gaze with studied coolness. "Yes, my lord?"

Falconer looked as if he meant to say something, and then a shuttered look stole into his eyes. "Nothing," he said, his voice as clipped as Ross's. "Will you be attending the ball at the Nethertons' tonight?"

Ross mentally reviewed the schedule his new secretary, a former sergeant in the Grays, had laid out for him. "Aye," he said, "I'll be there."

"Then we shall undoubtedly see one another there," Falconer replied with a cool nod. "Good day to you, my lord." And he walked quietly out of the room, leaving Ross to brood in solitary silence.

* * *

"Where *is* that wretch?" Addy paced the confines of the drawing room, pausing every few moments to glance out of the window. "He should have been here an hour ago!"

"Calm yourself, Adalaide," Aunt Matilda said from her seat before the fire. "St. Jerome is probably exhausted from all the running about he has been doing. And it's not as if today's lesson is so important it cannot wait."

That was true, although Addy was of no mind to admit as much. "That's hardly the point," she grumbled, her bottom lip thrusting forward in a decided pout. "A gentleman always keeps his word, and his lordship promised he would be here at eleven of the clock."

"Then perhaps something has detained him," Aunt Matilda soothed, making another stitch. "The papers are full of talk of another battle brewing in Spain. Likely he and the others are holding a council of war to decide what's to be done. You can't expect him to neglect his responsibilities to dance attendance upon you, you know."

Since the remark struck perilously close to home, Addy bristled in indignation. "I don't expect him to dance attendance upon me!" she declared, stumbling over the telling phrase. "The viscount is my pupil, not—not my beau!"

Aunt Matilda lowered her sewing to her lap and fixed Addy with her most censorious expression. "Then why are you in such a taking?" she asked bluntly. "His lordship is not the first of your pupils to forget a lesson, nor is he likely to be the last. You refine upon nothing, child, and one is left to wonder why."

Addy opened her lips, and then closed them after she thought better of it. Her aunt was too sharp by half, she admitted glumly, and returned to her pacing. Several of her pupils had missed lessons in the past, and she'd felt nothing other than a flash of annoyance. But in the six weeks since meeting the viscount she'd come to look forward to his visits, and the more she was in his company, the greater her desire to see him again.

It wasn't anything so silly as infatuation, she assured herself anxiously. Rather, it was respect for the sterling qualities that set his lordship apart from the other men in Society. He was a man like no other, and if her heart did beat a little faster at the sight of him, it was no one's business but her own. Or so she prayed. Another half-hour dragged inexorably past, and just as Addy was considering sending the viscount a very sharp note, she heard sounds coming from the hallway.

"Well, it is about time," she said, turning toward the door. She was rehearsing the scold she meant to read the viscount, when the door opened and the Earl of Hixworth came striding inside.

"Lord Hixworth," she said, swallowing her disappointment. "How lovely. To what do we owe the honor of this visit?"

He came to a halt, a look of mortification on his face. "Are—are we not to have our lessons today?" he asked, the confidence she'd taken such pains to instill in him melting away. "I—I can come back if I have mistaken the day."

Addy took instant pity upon him. "No, my lord,

you've not mistaken the day," she said, gliding forward to offer him her hand. "It is I who have mistaken the day. I quite forgot we were to work today on refusing invitations. As soon as Lord St. Jerome arrives, we shall begin."

"Oh, St. Jerome won't be joining us," Hixworth said, bobbing over her hand. "Saw him at Gentleman Jackson's this morning, and he asked that I bring along his apologies. Something's come up, don't you see?"

So her aunt was right, Addy thought, her heart warming at the thought of the viscount laboring on Wellington's behalf. "I quite understand," she told the earl, "I am sure events in Spain must have him occupied."

"Don't know about events in Spain," Hixworth said, hurrying over to bow over Aunt Matilda's hand. "He said he had an appointment with his tailor that he dared not miss. And then he and Denbury were going to the cockfights."

Addy's benevolence vanished. "Cockfights?" she echoed. "St. Jerome is missing our lessons for a cockfight?"

"Well, it is the pursuit of gentlemen, is it not?" Hixworth asked, all innocence as he took his chair. "Can't say I see the sense of watching chickens peck each other to death, but to each his own I do say. And, of course, one must never neglect one's obligation to his tailor."

"His obligation to his tailor? What about his obligation to me?" Addy all but howled the words. Here she'd thought Ross the most honorable man she'd ever met, and he'd tossed her aside for nothing more pressing than a vile sport and a simpering Frenchman. It was too much by half.

"He also asked that I tell you he shan't be able to call upon you for the rest of the week," Hixworth said, dutifully reciting the message he had been pledged to deliver. "His sincerest regrets, and all of that."

"Oh? And what is his excuse, if I may ask? An appointment with his glovemaker?" Addy snarled, more furious than she had ever been in her life.

Hixworth's brow knit in thought. "No, I do not believe so," he said in his ponderous manner. "He was going to the horse races, he said, and then he and Lord Falconer were promised at some house party or another. And of course there is his presentation at Almack's to prepare for. That's next week, don't you know."

Addy felt as if someone had kicked her legs out from beneath her. "No," she said carefully, "no, I did not. How did he accomplish that, do you know?"

"Well"—the earl leaned forward like an eager schoolboy about to share a delicious secret—"you must know his highness is mad for anything Scots. He has been patronizing the new Society that is starting up, and that is where he met St. Jerome. When he heard the tabbies at Almack's were dragging their feet offering him admittance, he invited the viscount to attend as his special guest. The moment the Patronesses heard that, they could not offer him a voucher fast enough. It was neatly done, eh?"

"Very neatly done," Addy echoed, fighting the urge to burst into tears. She'd worked for weeks to wrangle one of the coveted vouchers for Ross, and she'd meant to present it to him today. She'd been so proud of her efforts, and so happy to offer him the one thing he needed to achieve his goals. Now it seemed it had been for naught. He didn't need her help. He didn't need her.

"Are you all right, Miss Terrington?" Hixworth was regarding her anxiously. "You look a bit pale. Shall I ring for tea?"

Addy gave herself a mental shake. "No, my lord, thank you," she said, fastening a reassuring smile to her lips. "Well, if we needn't wait upon his lordship's leisure, I suppose we had ought to begin." And she hurled herself into the matter at hand, refusing to acknowledge the pain burning in her chest.

Over the next few days Addy did her best not to dwell on his lordship's defection. With the Season at its height she was kept busy attending various balls and entertainments, and if she occasionally looked for a certain blond head, she did not see anything amiss. The viscount had become something of a friend, and it was natural she would look for him. That she never seemed to encounter him bothered her more than a little, and by week's end her spirits were lower than they had ever been.

Keeping her unhappiness secret proved impossible. Several times Addy could feel her aunt's sharp gaze on her, but other than an occasional mutter under her breath, her aunt kept her own counsel. But as the days passed and Addy grew more withdrawn, it was plain the older woman had reached the end of her tether.

"Really, Adalaide, you are being foolish beyond permission," she scolded, giving Addy a stern scowl. "You'll be going into a decline next, swooning and sighing like a silly chit."

Addy stared down into the amber-tinted sherry in her

glass, refusing to let her aunt's sharp words overset her. "Nonsense, Aunt Matilda," she said, tossing back her head with pride. "I am not going into a decline. I am merely tired, that is all."

"Posh." Her aunt dismissed that with the contempt it deserved. "You've been moping about like a mother hen who's lost her last chick. You mustn't take it so hard, my dear. All birds must fly the nest at one time or another."

"I know that," Addy said, accepting the futility of pretending her current unhappiness had naught to do with his lordship. "It is just I feel St. Jerome is being precipitous about this. We aren't even halfway through my usual course of instruction, and there is so much more he needs to learn. I worry he has grown overconfident in his skills."

"What are you talking about?" her aunt demanded, clearly astonished. "The lad is the unqualified success of the Season! He is considered amongst the most eligible men in England, and tonight's presentation at Almack's will only make him that much more acceptable. I shouldn't wonder if he ends the Season engaged to the daughter of a duke!"

The thought of Ross, as she secretly thought of him, engaged sent another shaft of pain shooting through Addy. "That wasn't the purpose of his introduction to Society!" she said, her tone a tad sharper than she intended.

"No, but if it should happen, more to the better, I say," Aunt Matilda opined, settling back with her sherry and a smug smile. "You were forever after the lad about his responsibilities to the title, and everyone knows a lord's first duty is to produce more heirs. Let him marry some

nubile virgin and beget half a dozen or more little vis-
counts. Then we'll not have to worry about some other
half-wild Scotsman inheriting the title."

"His lordship isn't a half-wild Scotsman!" Addy cried,
bristling at the memory of the ugly whispers that had
been making the rounds. "Nor was he ever!"

"Don't be obtuse, my dear; of course he was half-
wild," Aunt Matilda said, shaking her head at Addy. "But
unfortunately, you have succeeded in civilizing him, and
more's the pity. He was far more interesting before you
got your hands upon him."

Addy glanced away at that, hurt by her aunt's teasing
words. Perhaps that was why Ross had stopped coming
about, she thought, nibbling on her bottom lip. She could
remember a dozen different times when he'd muttered
dark complaints, beneath his breath, and expressed the
resentment he bore the English for all he had suffered.
She was English . . . did that mean he resented her as
well?

But there was little time to brood as her brother, Arthur, and his pretty new bride, Alice, arrived to escort
them to Almack's. She was hardly fond of Arthur, finding his company trying at best, but tonight she was delighted to see him. His and Alice's presence would serve
to keep Aunt Matilda occupied, and that would give
Addy a few moments for herself. She had a great deal
of thinking to do.

As it was Wednesday, Almack's was crowded with
well-dressed people jockeying for power and position.
She'd always been privately amused by such obvious
posturing, thinking that as an intellectual she was far
above such behavior. Now she saw them simply as peo-

ple; no worse than she herself. Better, perhaps, because at least they were honest about their expectations.

She was secretly relieved when a furtive glance around the Assembly Room showed Ross had yet to appear. She did see Lord Hixworth, and was pleased when he came hurrying toward her. She was used to seeing him with a shy, slightly apologetic look upon his face, and she was somewhat taken aback to see an expression of dark indignation stamped there instead. He'd scarce reached her side before launching into furious speech.

"A disgrace, Miss Terrington, that is what it is! A dashed disgrace, and when I learn who is to blame for it, you may be quite certain I shall demand satisfaction!"

"Satisfaction for what, my lord?" she asked, her own troubles temporarily forgotten. She had never seen the young lord in such a state, and was curious to discover what might have gotten his back up. The only thing she knew him to care about so passionately was horseflesh, and she wondered if someone had sold him a stolen nag or some such thing.

"For the lies they are spreading about Lord St. Jerome!" he said, his eyes flashing in outrage. "It's all a hum, of course, as anyone who knows his lordship will happily testify. A finer and braver man I have yet to have the honor to meet, and I will not stand quietly by and see him slandered! Someone will pay for this, upon my word they will!"

Addy was delighted by such staunch loyalty to a friend, and gave his arm a reassuring pat. "It is good of you to be so concerned for his lordship," she told him with a smile. "But it's scarce something for which you need to call someone to account. 'Tis only gossip, after all."

"Do you mean to say you have already heard the rumors?" he gasped, his eyes wide with amazement. "I only heard them myself not five minutes ago! They're saying it is all over London!"

"And so it is," she agreed, thinking he was a dear, if slightly dotty, man. "But don't worry, as I said, 'tis only gossip and will quickly die. And if it contains an element of truth, well, then, no small matter. We—"

"What do you mean if it contains an element of truth?" He jerked away and was staring at her in horror. "Miss Terrington, never say *you* believe one word of these . . . scurrilous lies!"

Now it was Addy who stared at Lord Hixworth. "Well, not 'lies' per se," she said, wondering if the earl had perhaps been imbibing in something other than the club's infamous orgeat. "An exaggeration, or perhaps a cruel piece of snobbery, but—"

"A cruel piece of snobbery to label him a coward?" Hixworth said, his eyes flashing with the force of fury. "I should call it a great deal more than that! And as his friend, ma'am, I should think you would wish to do the same!"

Addy shook her head as if to clear it. "What are you talking about? Who is labeling Lord St. Jerome a coward?"

"Everyone!" Hixworth cried, his voice rising in his agitation. "Why do you think I am so angry? Someone has put it about that the viscount is a vile coward who was once court-martialed for desertion under fire! Do you not understand? He is ruined!"

Seven

Addy stared at Hixworth in stunned disbelief. "You're mad," she whispered, her stomach pitching wildly into her throat. "No one can possibly believe such lies!"

"That's what *I* said!" Hixworth retorted, and then waved his hand in dismissal. "But that's neither here nor there," he added, sounding surprisingly firm. "What's to be done about it, that's what is important."

"Where did you first hear the rumors?" Addy demanded, her earlier unhappiness forgotten as she turned her attention to the matter at hand.

"At my club. I stopped there before coming here, and it was all anyone could speak of. Those who know St. Jerome are doing their best to put an end to such tattle, but . . ." He shrugged.

"Do you know who started the talk?" Addy demanded, wondering if she could get a message to the Duke of Creshton. The whole thing smacked of political intrigue, and the wily old duke would best know how to deal with it.

"No one seems to know," Hixworth answered grimly. "Or if they do know, they're not saying. I quizzed one gentleman rather closely, and he would only say he'd had it from some captain newly returned from the Peninsula."

"The captain's name and regiment?" Addy's voice was clipped, even as her mind was racing ahead. Between her brothers and herself she had access to half the men in Whitehall, and it would be an easy matter to learn everything there was to know about this mysterious captain. Including, she thought coldly, whether the wretch had even *been* in Spain.

"He didn't say." Hixworth's tone made it plain he was far from pleased with the situation. "I've spoken with an old friend of mine who works in the Admiralty, and he's promised to help. It will take a while, but he can provide me with a list of officers traveling from Spain to Portsmouth. Once we have the devil's name, we will better know what's to be done."

"Have you heard?" Aunt Matilda rushed up to them, her eyes sparkling with temper. "You won't credit it, my dear, but they are saying Lord St. Jerome—"

"I know what they are saying," Addy interrupted, not wanting to hear the vile words, not even from her aunt. "We were just discussing what we should do."

"Do?" Aunt Matilda snapped. "I'll tell you what you shall do! You shall find whoever has been spreading these dreadful rumors, and then you shall have him horsewhipped!"

The earl's eyes frosted over and he thrust out his chin. "Believe me, Lady Fareham, if I learn who is responsible, I shall do a great deal more than whip the fellow; I shall slit his throat!" And with that he stalked off, leaving the ladies to stare after him in varying degrees of amazement.

"Well, the earl has come into his own, I must say," her aunt observed, nodding in satisfaction. "I knew St. Jerome would do the lad a world of good."

Addy didn't answer, her only concern for Ross. "Do you think the Patronesses know?" she demanded, reaching for her aunt's hand. "Will they deny him entrance?"

Her aunt's fingers closed comfortingly about hers. "Of course to the first, and I pray not to the second," she said, her faded gaze meeting Addy's. "He will be with the prince, thank heaven, and I do not think even that dreadful Mrs. Drummond Burrell has grown so toplofty she would risk offending a member of the royal household. Although to be honest, there is little I should put past that self-important creature."

The noise of the crowd, like the roar of the ocean, surrounded them, and Addy was so accustomed to it she scarce heard it anymore. But when that noise was cut, as swiftly as if a knife had been used, she was instantly aware. She stiffened in wariness, and was about to turn around when her aunt's fingers tightened around hers.

"It seems I can set your mind at ease on at least one score," she said, her voice strained despite the smile pinned to her lips. "Lord St. Jerome and the prince have just arrived."

Addy whirled around, her gaze going at once to the side of the room where a group of men were standing. She recognized Lords Creshton and Denbury, standing on either side of the prince and glancing about them with equally wary gazes. The prince was laced into a rich velvet jacket, a fortune in jewels glinting on his thick fingers and from the folds of his cravat. But even as she was studying the prince, her attention was fixed on Ross.

He was dressed in a severely cut jacket of black velvet, his muscular legs encased in the cream satin evening breeches the Patronesses declared *de rigueur* for the gentlemen. His dark blond hair was brushed back from his forehead, throwing the sharp bones of his face into prominence. His gaze, green as the emerald in his cravat, swept about the room, and she saw his eyes narrowing in cold awareness.

"What do you think we should do?" Aunt Matilda's hiss recalled Addy to the present. "Whatever it is, we'd best do it now. This lot will tear him to pieces."

Addy glanced back at Ross standing so brave and so alone. "We shall do what any good soldier does when confronted with the enemy," she said, her chin coming up in determination. "We shall attack." And without giving herself time to reconsider, she pushed her way through the silent crowd until she was standing before the prince and the rest of his party.

"Your royal highness," she said, curtsying gracefully despite the fact her legs were trembling with fear. "It is a pleasure to see you again."

In truth she and the prince had never met, but she was counting on the good sense he was reputed not to possess to keep him from revealing as much. He studied her for several seconds, and then inclined his head to her in regal condescension.

"Miss Terrington, we are delighted to see you looking so well," he said, as if greeting an old friend. "Pray tell us how we may be of assistance."

Addy hesitated, knowing everything rested on how she

handled the next several seconds. She took a few moments to send a brief prayer winging heavenward, and then gave the prince her most languid smile.

"You will not credit it, your highness," she said, unfurling her fan with studied indifference, "but there is the silliest tattle making the rounds just now."

A shrewd light entered the prince's pale blue eyes. "Indeed," he drawled coolly, "and pray what might those rumors be?"

Addy glanced at Ross in mute apology, and then back at the prince. It took all of her will, but she managed a fairly credible laugh. "That's what's so amusing, sir," she said, aware she was commanding the eyes of every person present. " 'They,' whoever the mysterious 'they' might be, are accusing St. Jerome of cowardice under fire."

There was a shocked gasp and the sound of one or two ladies engaging in swoons, and then a silence as heavy and thick as a winter fog settled over the Assembly Room. Addy could feel her heart pounding in her chest, but she refused to give in to her fear. To carry this off she had to act as if she considered the devastating rumor no more than a mildly amusing lark. To that end she wouldn't look at Ross. Couldn't. But she was aware of him, standing in rigid silence beside the prince.

Time trickled past at a snail's pace, and just as Addy was certain her desperate gamble had failed, the prince spoke again.

"Are they?" he asked, his lips twisting in well-born derision. "How singularly foolish of them. I cannot imagine anyone being so all about in the head as to believe such moonshine! Surely no person of breeding would be so deceived." He glanced about the knot of fascinated people clustered about them, and gestured imperiously at one of them.

"Lady Jersey," he said, indicating the haughty beauty with a bow. "What say you? *You* don't pay such talk any mind, do you?"

The pretty young woman's face was a study in conflicting emotions. She obviously had been set to give Ross the cut direct, and could not like having her small victory snatched away from her. On the other hand, she was too seasoned a campaigner not to realize she'd been outgunned and outmaneuvered by a superior foe. She cast Addy a fulminating glare before turning back to the prince.

"No, I do not, your highness," she said, her voice dripping with affected disdain. "Indeed, I shouldn't allow such foolish talk to even be mentioned here."

"Of course you would not," the prince said approvingly, beaming at her benevolently. "Such a sensible creature you are. You must walk with me, my dear," he added, offering her his arm with a low bow. "I enjoy having sensible creatures about me. It makes a most refreshing change, I vow."

With little choice but to accept, Lady Jersey stepped forward with a set smile on her lips. The prince turned toward the knot of waiting people, and Addy watched in amused admiration as he parted the crowd like Moses parting the Red Sea. She watched until they were gone, then turned to the men who stood flanking Ross in an unmistakable show of support.

"Gentleman," she said, including them all in her

bright smile, "the dancing is about to start. Shall we go?"

"A coward." Ross stood in front of the fireplace, his lips thinned with fury as he gazed down into the flames. "The world thinks I am a coward."

"Not the world," Adalaide corrected, her gentle voice washing over him like a soothing balm. "Only a small, very insignificant portion of that world."

Ross gave a bitter laugh. "Ah, but 'tis that insignificant portion whose opinion matters most," he said, turning to face her. "Was not the gaining of that opinion the reason for this? For all of this?" He indicated his elegant clothing with an impatient wave of his hand.

She bit her lip in obvious distress. "My lord, I—"

"Ross," he interrupted, leaving his post before the fire to join her on the settee. "Any soldier brave enough to ride into the cannon's mouth earns the right to call me by my given name."

In the golden light cast by the fire her skin gleamed like the rose-tinted pearls he'd found hidden in his uncle's safe. "I am not a soldier," she said, her gaze shifting away from his.

His smile warmed at her sudden modesty. "Are you not?" he asked softly, stroking a finger down the curve of her cheek. "You've the mind of one, and the heart. 'Twas a fine thing you did, Adalaide, and I'll not be forgetting it. *Míle buidheachas.*"

The husky words had her glancing back at him again. "What does that mean?" she asked curiously.

"A thousands thanks," he translated. " 'Tis that I owe

you, and a thousand more besides. Your plan was brilliant, *mo companach*. However did you think of it?"

Behind the lenses of her spectacles, her blue eyes danced with mischief. "Actually," she admitted, her lips curving in a smug smile, "I tried to think as I felt *you* would think. Attack first, rather than being taken unawares."

He nodded in agreement. "A good plan," he approved. "If a somewhat foolhardy one. What would you have done had the prince not been so quick to tumble to what you were about?"

She cocked her head to one side as if considering the matter. "Swooned," she said at last with a decisiveness that had him chuckling anew.

"I am glad it did not come to that," he said, recalling her disdain for such feminine theatrics. "Although now that I think on it, it might have been for the best if you had swooned."

Her russet-colored brows met in a tiny scowl of annoyance. "How do you mean?" she demanded, clearly puzzled by his words.

"Had you collapsed I should have had the perfect excuse for quitting that viper's nest," he explained with a shrug. "Then I might have been spared an evening of pretending I didn't feel the stares nor hear the accusing whispers of those about me."

There was a brief hesitation, and then Adalaide shocked him by laying her hand over his. "You might think me brave," she said, her tone level as her gaze met his. "But I think you are the one who is truly brave. I know what it cost you to know what they thought of you, and what it cost you to remain silent in the face of such ridiculous lies. But it was the only thing to be done. You do understand that, don't you?" She studied him anxiously.

"Aye," he said, and the truth of it was, he did. "Never surrender the field to the enemy."

"Just so," she said, looking relieved. "As the Bible says, 'The guilty fleeth where no man pursueth.' If we'd left, everyone would have assumed it was because we were ashamed or had something to hide. But because we stayed . . ."

"We looked as innocent as a nun at her prayers," he finished, frowning. "Perhaps. But you and the others are mad if you think this will be the end of it. You might have succeeded in stilling most of the gossip, but tongues will still wag regardless."

"I know," Adalaide said with a tiny sigh, "but at least this will give us time to find out who is behind the rumors. And as his grace said, once we have that information, we can best decide how to counter them."

Ross said nothing, thinking of the council of war that had broken up a few minutes earlier. After leaving Almack's he and the others had made straight for Miss Terrington's, where they'd spent the past two hours arguing and plotting their next move. The Duke of Creshton was convinced Wellington's enemies were behind the accusations, and because he had no counter-theory to offer, Ross was content to let the older man pursue the matter as he pleased. That didn't mean Ross didn't have his suspicions; suspicions he meant to keep to himself . . . for now.

"What will you do tomorrow?" Adalaide's brisk question brought Ross back to the present.

"What I'd planned to do, just as his grace suggested," he said calmly. "Falconer, Hixworth, and I are going to Newmarket for a day or so to watch the races. A tiresome sport, if you want my opinion of it," he added with a shrug. "When it comes to horses, I'd rather be riding one than watching it race down a track."

"What then?"

Ross mentally reviewed his schedule. "Visit a few gaming hells, drink myself into oblivion, flirt with the ladybirds—"

"Ladybirds!" Adalaide' s cheeks flamed with temper.

"Aye," Ross replied, all innocence at her indignant glare. " 'Tis a gentleman you mean me to be, and those are the pursuits of a gentleman, are they not?"

She studied him sharply for several seconds. "Are you twigging me?" she demanded in a tone so suspicious he was hard-pressed not to laugh.

"Perhaps a wee bit," he admitted, deciding to take a pity on her. "We are going to Newmarket, and a gaming hell or two while we're about it, I've no doubt. But I've never been one to indulge in strong drink, and as for the ladybirds"—he smiled wolfishly—"there are some things, Miss Terrington, a gentleman does not discuss with a lady."

"One thing I will say," he added before she could launch into the lecture she was clearly itching to read him, "is that I'll no longer allow the marquess to dictate where I go and who I see. I've kept away from you as he suggested, but I'm cursed if I will do again."

She gave a jerk of surprise, her blue eyes widening behind her spectacles. "Lord Falconer ordered you to stay away from me?"

"Aye." Ross simmered in resentment as he recalled the conversation. "He felt if I was seen too much in your company, it would give credence to the gossip I was the sow's ear you were trying to make into a silk purse. Of course," he said, giving a harsh laugh, "that was before we learned the *ton* had found other things to occupy their useless tongues."

"What is it?" he demanded when she continued staring at him in silence. "Are you saying you didn't notice my absence? You surprise me, Miss Terrington. I thought you would be after me for dereliction of duty."

She glanced away from him, her slender fingers threading together. "I noticed," she admitted softly, "but I thought . . ."

"Thought what?" he pressed, reaching out to lift up her chin so their gazes were once more meeting. "Come, Adalaide," he pressed gently. "We've too much between us for you to turn proper on me now. Tell me what you thought."

He didn't think she would answer, but she said, "I thought you didn't feel in need of further instruction."

He blinked at the response. "Perhaps I did feel that," he admitted, frowning, "but you should have known I would still have continued calling upon you if 'twas possible. You and your aunt were my first true friends here, and I should never have turned my back upon you as if I had no further use for you."

"I—I suppose I did think it strange when you did not call," she said after a few moments. "But then I thought perhaps I had offended you, or that you disliked me because I am . . ."

"Am what?" He all but shouted the words, maddened

by her reticence. From the first, she had nagged, lectured, and badgered him, but now that he most needed to know her thoughts, she had turned mute as a statue. *The devil take the woman!* he thought with a scowl. Would she never react as he expected she would?

"English!" She flung the word at him. "I am English, and you have never been hesitant letting your opinion of us be known! You hate us, don't you?"

"What are you talking about?" he said, honestly perplexed by her accusation. "How can I say I hate the English when I've spent near to half my life fighting and killing for them?"

"You might have fought for us," Adalaide agreed, her head held high as she met his outraged glare, "and there is no doubting you're doing your duty and more to help Wellington. But the simple truth of the matter is that you don't really like us. Do you, my lord?"

Faced with such a blunt demand for the truth, Ross could be no more than honest.

"No," he said wearily, and this time it was he who glanced away from her. "No, I do not." He rose to his feet and began pacing. He walked back to the fireplace, staring down once more into the flames as he struggled for words so raw and painful he seldom allowed himself to even think them.

" 'Tis not just because I am Scots," he said, his gaze on the flames but his mind thousands of miles away. "That is the greatest part to be sure, but still only a part. When I enlisted as a common soldier and was sent off first to India and then to Egypt, I saw the flower of English manhood, and it sickened me. The men I saw were not men at all, but childish brutes who thought themselves the superiors of everyone and everything else. We weren't even human to them, merely mindless animals to be starved and beaten into submission."

"Ross." Addy's voice was filled with anguish as she rose to join him at his lonely post. "I am so sorry . . ."

"I've been flogged," he said, ignoring her soft words. "And threatened with court-martial, by the way, although not for cowardice. Do you want to know what my crime was?" he asked, lifting his head to meet her gaze. "Do you want to know what I did that had me standing in danger of losing my life?"

"What did you do?"

"It was in Egypt," he said, his voice raw with pain. "I was half dead from the fever, along with most of the regiment, and our lieutenant, a pimply-faced, plump little fellow all of twenty, decided we needed drilling. I was a corporal then, but in charge of the company because our sergeant was too ill to leave his pallet. I explained to the lieutenant that we were all sick from the fever, and that it was decent food and medication we were needing, not a lot of useless parading. The lieutenant then demanded I have the men muster up, and when I refused, I was flogged and then thrown into the stockade."

"Why were you not charged?"

"Because the lieutenant sickened and died of the same fever within two days' time," Ross said, a bitter smile twisting his lips at the irony of the young man's death. "The captain allowed the matter to drop because the regiment had just received orders to set sail for the Peninsula. I might be a disloyal bastard of a Scotsman, he told me, but I was a soldier, and as such I was needed in Spain. He also said that if God was just I would soon be killed. Apparently God was not so just. The captain fell at Talavera, not five weeks later."

An appalled silence greeted his words, and when he looked at Adalaide, he saw her beautiful eyes filled with tears. "Ah, *annsachd*," he whispered, brushing the tears away with a finger that was none too steady. "No tears. I did no' speak of these things to make you cry."

"I know," she said, her bottom lip trembling. "That's what makes me want to cry all the more, and I *hate* crying."

She sounded so truculent, so like the overbearing little martinet he had first come to know, he couldn't help but chuckle. "And why is that?" he asked, his voice soft as he brushed another tear away. "Tears are a woman's greatest weapon, little one, for they make even the strongest men want to crawl."

Her expression grew stormy. "I don't want to see you crawl!" she exclaimed, her tone surprisingly fierce. "I never want to see you crawl, do you hear me, you wretch?"

Ross could only stare at her, torn by the desire to laugh, and by another desire that didn't bear close scrutiny. "Aye, *annsachd*," he said with false meekness, "I hear you."

"And don' t call me names when I don't know what they mean!" she added, scowling. "I hate not knowing what you are saying."

"Yes, *an*—yes, Miss Terrington." He was grinning like a fool. "As you wish."

"Oh!" She batted his hand away. "Why do I even bother? This will teach me the folly of feeling pity for such a thickheaded, arrogant scoundrel! Now, what are we going to do about these rumors? I know his grace and Lord Falconer have the situation well in hand, but I want to do something as well."

The abrupt shift in conversation had him blinking in confusion, but he grudgingly followed her lead. "You've done enough, Adalaide," he told her, not wanting her to put her reputation at any more risk than she had already done. "The rest is better left to us. We will take care of the matter, have no doubt about that."

"But I want to help," she insisted, clearly refusing to be set aside. "My brothers have several friends in the government, and I am sure if I asked they would be happy to do some nosing about. If General Wellington's foes are to blame for this, then the sooner we mount a counteroffensive, the better."

He raised his eyebrows at that. "So you think to lecture me about warfare, do you?" he asked, his tone mild.

She gave him a regal look. "And if I do?"

"Then I would remind you, lass, that the first rule of engagement is never to assume anything," he told her bluntly. "The enemy you are seeking could be right there beside you, and you'd not even suspect it until they were slitting your throat."

"What is that supposed to mean?"

He started answering, but then thought better of it. He had no real proof, and until he did, he didn't want to tip his hand to his cousin. If Adalaide even suspected Atherton was involved, he didn't doubt but that she would march up to him and box his ears good and proper. A woman who would confront a prince would dare anything; the thought had him trembling with fear.

"Never mind," he told her firmly. "And I meant what

I said about your keeping clear of this. 'Tis my reputation, Adalaide, and I'll be the one to save it. Mind you remember that, you little *briosag,* or I shall make you most heartily sorry for it."

She raised her chin with cool pride. "I have asked you not to use foreign words when addressing me," she reminded him, her tone imperious as a queen's.

" 'Tis not foreign," he said, chuckling at what he considered her shameful ignorance. " 'Tis Gaelic, and there are some words you're better off not knowing the meaning of." While she was mulling over what that might mean, he grabbed her hand and raised it to his lips for a playful kiss.

"Keep yourself out of mischief, *annsachd,*" he told her, his eyes dancing as she jerked her hand free of his. "I promise I'll call upon you when I am back in London." He turned to go, and had almost reached the door when she came scurrying after him.

"Wait!" she cried. "Tell me what that word means!"

He turned to grin at her. "Which word?" he asked, feigning innocence. *"Annsachd?"*

"Yes." She glared up at him defiantly. "Is it an insult?"

He considered how best to answer that. "Hardly," he drawled, resisting the urge to show her the endearment's true meaning. " 'Tis . . . a compliment, I suppose you might say. It means dearest friend, amongst other things."

"Oh." Her brows met in thought as she mulled his response over in her mind. "And the other word? *Briosag?* What is its meaning?"

He hid a wince at her pronunciation. "Oh, that one,"

he said, wondering if he could make it safely out the door before she was on him like a fury.

"Yes, that one." She had folded her arms under her pretty breasts and was glaring at him like a suspicious wife. "What is its meaning? Or are you going to pretend it hasn't a meaning?" she added when he remained silent.

"Oh, all words have their meanings, *annsachd*," he assured her, tongue in cheek. "Some more than others."

"Then what does it mean?" She all but howled the words at him.

He opened the door, making sure her aunt and several of the servants were in sight before turning back to grin at her.

"Witch," he said, and then stepped out into the hall, closing the door on her shriek of outrage.

Eight

"That's the last of them, thank heavens. I've looked through every one of the morning journals, and there's not one mention of last night's incident in any of them," Aunt Matilda said, smiling up at Addy from the mound of papers piled before her plate at the breakfast table. "Congratulations, child, it seems your gamble has worked after all."

"Thank you, Aunt," Addy said, managing a half smile for the older lady's benefit. "But there are still the afternoon papers to be got through, and they are all controlled by the Whigs."

"Well, then, we shall simply have to deal with them when the time comes," Aunt Matilda said with a brisk nod. "Which reminds me, my dear, at what time may we expect his lordship and the others? I've been thinking, and there are several things about last night I should like to discuss with them."

Addy hastily picked up her cup. "I'm afraid Lord St. Jerome shan't be calling today, Aunt," she said with a forced air of indifference. "He told me last night he and

Lord Falconer were going up to Newmarket for the races."

"Heavens, has the racing season started already?" her aunt asked, nibbling thoughtfully on a bite of roll. "I had no idea the year was so far gone as that. Ah, well, that is how it is when one gets old. Time drags on forever when one is your age, and then flies past in the wink of an eye when one is mine."

And on she chatted, offering comment or complaint about any number of topics while Addy sat in dutiful silence. It was as well Aunt expected so little of her audience, Addy mused, listening as her aunt rattled on about the princess's latest *imbroglio*. Addy's head was so stuffed with cotton batting, she didn't think she would be capable of logical discourse.

This was all Ross's fault, she decided, poking at her eggs in incipient resentment. If the dratted man hadn't thrown her into such turmoil, she would never have spent the great part of the night staring up at the ceiling and wondering about things best left unthought. Her heart had ached when she remembered the stark way he had described his days in the Army, and more than once she'd found herself wiping away tears. Those experiences explained much of the hard and aloof man she'd come to know, but oh! how she hated the thought of them. But that wasn't the only thing that had kept her awake long into the night.

It had been the memory of the way he had touched her, his hands so gentle as he'd wiped away her tears. He'd been standing so close to her she could feel the warmth of his body, and the softness of his breath feathering across her cheeks. There'd been a moment while he'd been cupping her face between his hands, his eyes gazing down into hers, when she'd hoped he was going to kiss her. Her heart had been racing like a mad thing in her breast, and a delicious warmth had stolen over her. She remembered the way her knees had trembled, and the way her lashes seemed so heavy they—

"Adalaide!"

"What?" Addy jolted upright, her heart pounding and a hectic flush staining her cheeks. She glanced at her aunt, and found the older lady regarding her with a knowing smirk on her face.

"I am sorry, Aunt Matilda," she said, straightening her spectacles and striving for nonchalance. "What did you say?"

Her aunt stared at her for several more seconds before her lips curled in a crafty smile. "Nothing so important it cannot wait," she said, gesturing to the hovering footman. "Have some coffee, my dear. You must have cobwebs in your mind, for all the attention you are paying."

Addy waited until the footman had served her and retreated to the kitchens before speaking again.

"This is much better, Aunt. Thank you," she said, taking a grateful sip of the richly flavored coffee. "Now, what was it you were you saying? I promise to pay attention this time."

"I was reminding you we are supposed to be meeting with the Wellfords this afternoon," her aunt said. "Their son, Richard, is in the midst of his fifth Season, and making a sad hash of it for all I can understand. The lad is so bookish he won't say a word to a lady but to quote Latin at her. They are hoping you will prove as successful with him as you have with all the others."

Addy set her cup on its saucer. "I'm not certain if I ought to be taking on another pupil, Aunt. Admittedly Lord Hixworth has improved far beyond my expectations, but I've still a great deal left to teach him. And with this new business with Lord St. Jerome, I really haven' t the time to dedicate to a new pupil."

"Nonsense," her aunt said with a scowl. "The earl is all but ready to fly out on his own, and the viscount, this dreadful business notwithstanding, has no need of your expertise whatsoever. It would be selfish of you to deny the Wellfords the benefits of your instruction."

Addy winced inwardly at her aunt's blunt words. However hurtful they were, they were nonetheless the truth. Ross did have no further use for her, and perhaps it was past time she was admitting as much. It would make it so much easier when the time came to watch him walk away.

"Are the Wellfords so far in the suds, then?" she asked curiously, knowing it was the desperate need for an advantageous match that brought most of her students to her doorstep.

"Heavens, no!" her aunt replied. "Rather the opposite, in fact. Mr. Wellford has made a tidy sum in the China trade. But he is the only male remaining in his family, and Richard is his only son. If the lad doesn't get married soon and beget an heir, as poor Mr. Wellford fears he will not, the entire Wellford line will die out! We really cannot let that happen, Adalaide, indeed we cannot."

Addy considered the matter for a few seconds before reaching her decision. Perhaps a new challenge was just what she needed to get her mind off . . . other things.

And as her aunt had pointed out, it was her duty to help families like the Wellfords. "Very well, ma'am," she said, her heart lifting somewhat. "I suppose I might be willing to give the younger Mr. Wellford whatever help I can."

"However," she added, bending a stern look on the older woman, "I want it understood I still mean to carry out my mission for Lord Wellington. You and St. Jerome might consider he stands in no need of my tutelage, but I am far from finished with him. Until this business with the rumors is resolved, I shall still consider him my pupil."

"But I thought St. Jerome said you were to stay out of this!" her aunt protested, and then immediately clamped her lips closed.

It took Addy less than a second to discern the reason for her aunt's discomfiture. "Aunt Matilda, have you been listening at keyholes again?" she demanded suspiciously.

Knowing her aunt as she did, Addy could swear she heard the wheels in the other woman's head turning as she weighed which approach would best serve.

"Of course," her aunt said, evidently deciding that having been caught red-handed, her best defense lay in boldly confessing her crime. "And you needn't look so outraged, young lady," she added at Addy's disapproving frown. "Five and twenty you might be, but I am still your chaperon. I should have been very behind-hand in my duties to leave you alone with a man without making sure of your reputation! Indeed, I am shocked you should even suggest such a thing."

Despite her indignation, Addy was forced to admit to

a reluctant admiration for her aunt's shameless manipu-
lation. "How much did you hear?" she asked, struggling
not to smile.

"Enough," Aunt Matilda admitted, sobering. "Poor
lad, he has had a hard time of it, has he not? Small
wonder he seems such a cold fish at times.

"But really, Adalaide," she continued, shaking her
head at Addy in disappointment, "what could you have
been thinking? His lordship was all set to kiss you, and
what must you do but fly up into the boughs at him!"

"Aunt Matilda!"

"What?" Her aunt gave a haughty sniff at Addy's horrified gasp. "I might be in my dotage now, but don't
forget I was once a young maid like you. There the pair
of you were standing not inches from one another; it was
the perfect opportunity for him to steal a kiss. And he
would have, if you hadn't lost your nerve there at the
end."

Addy opened her lips in furious defense, and then
thought of something. "And you saw all of this from a
keyhole?"

"And the priest's hole on the other side of the drawing
room," her aunt confessed with singular want of remorse. "My husband showed it to me when he bought
me this house. I must say I was finally happy for the
chance to put it to use."

"Madam, you are the most complete—"

"Pray don't be stuffy, Adalaide," the other woman
said, interrupting Addy's indignant sputtering. "You put
me uncomfortably in mind of Reginald's wife when you
do, and you know I can't abide the creature above five
minutes' time. She gives me the megrims."

"Now, as to St. Jerome," she plowed on, "faint heart, as they say, never won fair lady, or in this case, fair gentleman. If you are going to win St. Jerome you're going to have to do a far better job of it than you've done to date. But never fear." She winked at Addy. "Auntie Matilda will be happy to help you."

"But I don't want his lordship!" Addy cried in frustration.

"Of course you do," her aunt said, waving aside Addy's objection as if of little importance. "The lad is rich, handsome, titled, and quite the most honorable man I have ever met. You would be particular beyond all enduring to turn your nose up at such a catch."

"But no more of that," she said hastily. "The Wellfords will be here within a few hours, and here we are still in are morning gowns. What will your curriculum be this time, hmm? From all accounts the lad will need all you have to offer, and likely a great deal more."

The meeting with the Wellfords went better than Addy might have hoped. The younger Mr. Wellford was indeed quite bookish, but also endearingly shy and possessed of a singularly sweet nature that made Addy realize he would be quite wasted on the *ton*. Instead she decided she would see him introduced in some of the more intellectual circles where she moved, certain one of her bluestocking friends would find the agreeable young man of particular interest. She even had a certain friend in mind, and after making arrangements to give the younger man some quick lessons in flirting and social conversation, Addy sent the family on its way.

The rest of the day was given over to handling the mound of invitations and letters that had arrived in the afternoon post. To her amazement she found herself being regarded as something of a heroine, and nearly every letter praised not only her, but Ross as well. Several were from men who had served with him on the Peninsula, and each of them offered her whatever help she required in defending Ross's reputation.

In her orderly fashion she made a list of the names and set it aside. Ross might have decreed she was not to involve herself in the matter, but that didn't mean she had to obey him. Besides, she decided primly, there was nothing wrong with her writing the gentlemen to thank them for their generous offers.

They were promised that night at the home of Lady Hillburoughs, one of her aunt's oldest friends. There was to be dancing, and as was her custom, Addy set out for the dowagers' corner, were she passed most evenings at such events. She never made it. The moment she arrived, she was surrounded by a wall of men all desirous of making her acquaintance.

"Served with the sergeant in Spain, don't you know," one tanned young man explained, bowing over her hand. "A braver, finer man I've yet to meet, enlisted or officer. When I heard what was being said, I was ready to do murder."

"As was I," another man interposed. "I was there at Fuentes D'Onoro, and I'd have been killed if a company of Rifles, led by Sergeant MacCailan, hadn't rushed forward in a charge. He ought to have been promoted then, if you want my opinion."

And on it went. Addy spent the next hour being

treated to various stories of Ross's bravery. It quickly became obvious to her that while he might have held a low opinion of the majority of English officers, it was an opinion that wasn't returned by those same officers. To a man they were vociferous in their defense of Ross, and they were equally vociferous in pledging their undying loyalty to her. It was a novel experience to be the focal point of so much male ardor, and Addy was surprised to find she was feminine enough to enjoy the feeling.

Finally she was able to extract herself from their midst, only to be swallowed up by another group comprised mostly of females, all eager to declare her their *dearest* friend. Shedding herself of them proved a little more difficult, but at last she managed to slip away. Hoping for a few minutes' respite in which to mull over all that had occurred, she hurried to the farthest corner of the room where a lone footman was dispensing fruit punch and other delicacies. She'd barely taken her first sip when she felt someone touch her arm and turning, found herself face-to-face with William Atherton.

"My dear Miss Terrington, what an unexpected delight to encounter you," he said, making a great show of bowing over her hand. "I was hoping we might have cause to meet."

"Were you, Mr. Atherton?" she asked, taking the man's measure in a single, haughty glance. "Might one ask why?"

His thick lips thinned at the obvious set down in her voice. "To thank you, of course," he said, his dark eyes narrowing as he studied her. "These days I might not fly in quite so elevated circles as you and my esteemed cousin, but even I heard of your daring championing of him. It was quite good of you."

Addy took immediate offense to the sneering note in his voice. "It is hardly 'good,' Mr. Atherton, to defend an innocent man against such cowardly and vicious lies," she informed him in her most imperious manner. "And as it happens, his lordship hardly stands in need of my poor efforts."

A hard look stole into his mud-colored eyes. "Indeed?"

Addy considered dumping the contents of her cup over his head, before deciding it would be a foolish waste of punch. There were other ways of dealing with the odious toad, and she was just of a mind to employ them.

"Do you see the two men over there, the ones in uniforms of the Guard?" she asked, turning to nod at two of the men she had been speaking with less than half an hour earlier.

"Yes," Mr. Atherton responded cautiously.

"They are just returned from Spain," she explained sweetly. "The one on the left, Major Kelmston, served with your cousin at Ciudad Rodrigo, and he tells me your cousin led the first assault into the fort, despite the fact that he had sustained several shrapnel wounds. The other man is Colonel Adamsleigh. He confided to me that he is here on Wellington's behalf to bestow a commission on his lordship."

"A *field* commission," she stressed, fixing him with a satisfied smile. "One earned for bravery in the face of enemy action. So you see, Mr. Atherton, Lord St. Jerome had no need of my defending him. His actions have already done so; loudly and in a way that should put an end to such ill-bred rumors once and for all. Do you not agree?"

He drew himself up stiffly, enmity fairly dripping from every pore. "Indeed, Miss Terrington, I do," he said, his tone clipped. "If you will pardon me, the music is starting and I must find my partner for this next set. Good evening to you."

Addy watched him stalk away, her eyes narrowing in sudden speculation. Perhaps they'd been going about this the wrong way, she thought. Given the importance of his lordship's mission, it had seemed most logical to assume the attack on his reputation had political implications. But what if there were a simpler, more basic motivation behind the rumors? What if—

Someone touched her arm.

Devil take it! Addy's temper flared to life. Was she not to know even one moment's peace during this blasted night? She firmed her jaw and whirled around, prepared to give whatever poor soul stood there a piece of her mind. Instead her jaw dropped, her eyes widening in incredulity as she gaped at the elegantly dressed man standing before her.

"Ross!" she gasped, his given name slipping from her lips. "Whatever are you doing here?"

Ross glared down at Adalaide in fury. He'd been searching for her the better part of a quarter hour, and when he finally found her she was jawing pleasantly away with his plague of a cousin. Under ordinary circumstances he might have been willing to overlook her questionable choice of companions, but with knowledge

of his cousin's perfidy fresh in his mind, he found he
could not be so sanguine. Instead, he said the first words
to pop into his mind.

"The Good Lord take you for a fool, madam! What
the bloody devil do you think you're about talking to that
deamhan?"

Her small jaw thrust out at once, her dark blue eyes
icing over with displeasure as she boldly met his gaze.
"I beg your pardon, Lord St. Jerome," she said in a tone
better suited to a dowager three times her young years.
"Are you addressing me?"

Lord St. Jerome, he noted, his temper simmering.
When she'd first seen him she'd called him by his given
name. No matter, he decided darkly; they would resolve
that later. In the meanwhile there was something else
that needed saying.

"Aye, Miss Terrington, I was," he said, his accent
thick with fury. Without stopping to weigh the consequences of his actions, he reached out to capture her
slender wrist in his hand.

"A word with you, if I might," he growled, and without waiting for a response he turned and half dragged,
half led her away.

The other guests were occupied with dancing and gossiping, so there was no one to notice and whisper. Angry
Ross might be, but not so angry he would gleefully leap
into the morass of yet another scandal. Seeking privacy
for all he had to say, he led her out into the gardens, and
when he was certain they were private, he turned to face
her.

"Very well," he said, releasing her arm and glaring
down at her in displeasure. "I am waiting."

Her response was to shove her glasses back on her nose and angle her chin up at its most pugnacious angle. "Then, sir, you shall wait until Doomsday has come and gone," she informed him in defiant tones. "I've no intention of saying another word." And she folded her arms across her chest.

The situation was as dire as anything he could imagine, but that didn't stop Ross from chuckling at her heated threat. "Don't be foolish, *annsachd*," he said, resisting the urge to kiss her sulky mouth. "You couldn't remain silent to save your soul."

"Oh!" Her arms dropped and her hands tightened into fists. "Of all the arrogant—"

"There," he interrupted, grinning at her, "you see? Not ten seconds did you let pass before you were after lecturing me. Now stop with your fussing, Adalaide, and tell me why you were talking to my cousin."

She hesitated, and then gave a long-suffering sigh. "I was talking to him because he was talking to me," she said, the patience in her voice making it plain she was but humoring him.

"Was he?" Ross considered that. "About what?"

"You. He said he wished to thank me for last evening. That reminds me"—she gave him another scowl—"why *are* you here? I thought you and Lord Falconer were bound for Newmarket."

"We were," he replied simply. "Now we're not. Tell me more about my cousin. What else did he say?"

She jerked her shoulders in a shrug, and he noticed her gaze no longer met his. "Nothing. It is just as I told you. He said he wanted to thank me, and that was the end of that."

"Adalaide," he began, his voice gentle, "what is it you're not telling me? I know you, and I know when you're telling the truth and when you're not."

Her head came up in indignation. "That is the truth!"

"A piece of it, perhaps," he agreed, nodding, "but not all. And I need to know all. Tell me precisely what he said."

She chewed her lip, her gaze worried behind the lenses of her spectacles. "He did say he wanted to thank me," she admitted reluctantly, "but there was something in his voice, something that made me wonder if . . ."

"If he was the one behind the rumors," Ross finished, not surprised she'd already tumbled to a truth he and the others had spent the day uncovering. "Aye, I know. I learned of it just as we were getting ready to leave London. That is why we decided to postpone our journey."

"What will you do about it?" She moved closer to him, her hand gentle as it covered his.

"Nothing," he replied with a harsh laugh. "I'd like to call him out and kill him for staining my honor so, but I cannot. 'Twould cause a scandal, I'm told, and heaven knows we mustn't have a scandal."

"I'm sorry, Ross."

Her soft tones soothed, almost enough to heal the bitterness bubbling up inside him. "As am I," he said, covering her hand with his own. "I was even willing to compromise, and would have been content to beat him to a bloody pulp and make him eat every one of his foul lies, but Falconer said even that would not do. In the end it came down to a choice between my name and my duty, and I knew which one must take precedence. So I am to remain a branded coward." He laughed again to keep from cursing. "Well, no matter. I've been called worse and lived to tell the tale."

"You're not a coward!" Her fingers tightened on his arm, her expression turning sweetly fierce in his defense. "No one who matters thinks so! Why, you're even to be offered a field commission! If that isn't enough to satisfy the gossip-mongers, then to the devil with them. You're ten times more a man than any of them could ever hope to be!"

The passionate declaration made Ross's heart stop, and when it started beating again, it was with an intensity that had the pulses pounding through his body. "Am I?"

"Of course you are!" she insisted, her creamy cheeks flushed with emotion. Above the prim decolletage of her gray silk ball gown, the soft swell of her breasts rose and fell with her breathing, and the sight of them put paid to Ross's resolve.

"Then why don't you treat me as a man?" he asked, tracing a gentle finger across the lush bow of her lip.

"I—I do," she stammered, her lip trembling beneath his touch. "I treat you exactly as I treat the others."

"Aye," he agreed, slipping his arm about her waist and drawing her against him. "Like a wee lad in short pants to be told yes or no, to do this and not to do that. You scold me, you lecture me, but you never treat me as a man would be treated by a woman."

Her gaze fell from his, and Ross steeled himself to be pushed away. Instead, Adalaide raised her head, her eyes meeting his with a directness that was both bold and shy at the same time.

"Perhaps that is because you never treat me as a man

would treat a woman," she said, her voice so soft he had to bend his head to catch the whispered words.

He froze for an instant, and then his hand slipped down to cup her chin, turning her face up to his. "Are you saying that is how you wish to be treated?" he asked, knowing that by asking the question he would be stepping over a line from which there could be no retreat.

Her gaze continued holding his, resolution shimmering in her jewel-colored depths. "Yes," she said, sounding as certain of herself as she did when issuing her orders. "Yes, that is what I am saying."

He gazed down into her face for several more seconds, and then he felt a warm glow of delight spreading through him. "Very well, Miss Terrington," he drawled, his lips curving into a smile as he drew her further into his arms. "As you wish." And with that he lowered his head, his mouth covering hers in a kiss of ardent demand.

Nine

The taste of Adalaide's lips was sweeter than any wine Ross had ever drunk, and every bit as intoxicating. He drank from them thirstily, his senses swimming with drunken pleasure. Her mouth was as lush and soft as he'd dreamed it would be, and when his tongue flicked over her lips in hungry demand, she responded with a soft moan of wonder.

"Adalaide." He raised his mouth from hers to breathe her name in a voice made hoarse from passion. *"Annsachd,* open your lips for me. Let me kiss you as I have longed to kiss you."

He lowered his mouth to hers once more, and was delighted when her lips parted beneath the onslaught of his own. His tongue surged eagerly into her mouth, and his body hardened in response to the warmth and the sweetness he found there. He longed for more, for so much more from her, but even in the heat of his hunger he knew he could not have it. Shuddering, he drew back, his breath ragged in his chest as he fought for a control that had never seemed so far away.

"We must stop, *leannan,*" he whispered, laying his forehead against hers. "Else I fear we'll not be able to stop."

She gazed up at him, her eyes dazed and her lips moist and red from the heat of his kisses. "Ross, I—"

"Hush." He laid his finger over her lips, knowing if she should say even one word in remorse for what they had shared, it would shatter what remained of his heart. " 'Tis but a kiss, Adalaide," he added, forcing a note of lightness into his voice. "A kiss between a man and a woman under the moonlight, and nothing else. Now let us return to the ballroom, or it will be another scandal we're making out here amongst the roses. Come."

To his relief she did as he asked, slipping her hand into his arm and walking at his side as coolly as if they were strolling down Bond Street in the bright light of day. They'd almost reached the doors to the ballroom before she spoke again.

"You never did say, my lord, how you discovered your cousin was behind the rumors," she said, flicking him a curious look.

"Actually 'twas Elliott who uncovered the truth for us," Ross answered, annoyed she should turn so primly formal so easily. "He was up the better part of the night, poking about and asking questions of all he could before learning those spreading the rumors could trace the source back to one man."

"Mr. Atherton." She nodded, her mouth firming in distaste. She was silent another moment before shooting him another quizzing look. "Who is Elliott, if I may ask? Another friend from your days in the Army?"

" 'Tis Hixworth," he said, drawing her to a halt. "Do

you not know your own students' names?" he asked, unable to resist the urge to tease her. "For shame, Miss Terrington. I thought you a far better instructress than that."

To his delight, her eyes flashed with immediate temper. "Of course I knew his Christian name was Elliott," she said, her tone so starchy he was hard-pressed not to kiss her again. "But it would have been most improper for me to address him in so casual a manner."

"Aye, and so it would," he said, chuckling. They were at the door now, and through it he could hear the sound of laughter and music. He knew he should let her go, but he was loath to do so. Eager to delay the inevitable if only for a few minutes, he said something he'd been wanting to say for a very long while. Turning to her, he flashed her a teasing smile.

"Do you know, Miss Terrington, what I thought the very first time I clapped eyes on you?"

She looked curious, and then a warm glow of color infused her face as she apparently recalled that the first place he had seen her was in his bedchamber. "I am sure I do not," she said, her eyes fixed at a point somewhere over his shoulder. "And furthermore it is not something we should speak of considering the . . . irregularity of the situation."

"That I was in my bed, do you mean?" he asked, all innocence as she glared up at him. "No matter. What I thought, Miss Terrington," he continued, "was that you looked like an elf. What the crofters call a *sithiche,* a mischievous sprite come from the glens to lead me back the Low Road to the Highlands. Then you opened your lips to bark orders and questions at me, and I was certain

you were a *tannasg* instead, come to pester me into perdition. In the days since, I've come to think I was right."

Her cheeks flushed brighter with indignation. "I'm
not so bad as that!"

"Aye, lass." He grinned, carrying her hand up to his
lips for another kiss. "You are. But do not worry yourself over it. I am a soldier, and used to fighting for what
I want. Now come, I am sure your aunt must be wondering where you've gone."

An elf. The dratted man thought she looked like an
elf. Adalaide paced the confines of her moonlit bedchamber, her hair streaming in wild disarray about her
shoulders. Behind her the bedsheets lay all tangled, mute
testimony to her valiant battle for sleep. In the end frustration and confusion had overcome exhaustion, and
she'd abandoned her bed with a disgruntled mutter. Be-
damned if she'd spend another night staring up at the
ceiling like some heroine in a Gothic, she thought sourly.

Ross had kissed her. The thought brought her to a halt
in the center of her room. Her eyes drifted shut, her hand
trembling as she raised her fingers to touch her lips.
They still felt warm, tender, and she was almost certain
they still bore Ross's taste. The sensual thought had her
eyes popping open in chagrin.

What nonsense! she told herself, resuming her pacing.
She was being foolish beyond permission, and there was
no excuse for such behavior. It wasn't the first time she'd
been kissed, nor even, if she was to be completely honest, was it the first kiss she'd found enjoyable. She

wasn't quite such an antidote as to eschew all male companionship. It was simply that. . . .

It was simply that this was the first kiss to make her want *more,* she admitted, her heart racing with the heady emotion she recognized as desire. It had made her long to touch Ross, and to have him touch her in ways she'd only heard whispered of. A virgin she might be, but she'd been out in Society long enough to know of what went on between a man and a woman. Until now she'd regarded the prospect of lovemaking with cool disinterest; curious, but also certain she was above such things. Now she hungered in ways she'd never hungered before, and she both rejoiced and despaired in her newfound emotions.

" 'Tis but a kiss, Adalaide." Ross's husky murmur came back to haunt her. *"A kiss and nothing else."* The words had been like a sword thrust into her very soul, but she knew he'd meant them as both comfort and a warning. Comfort to assure her he would not ask more from her than the touching of their lips, and a warning, she supposed, lest she think the kiss a form of declaration. He might like her and desire her in the physical sense, but that was all it could ever be. He would never marry her, and he had too much honor and she too much pride for there to be any question of any other sort of relationship between them. Disheartened at the admission, she returned to her bed.

Tomorrow, she told herself, pulling the covers up to her chin and curling into a tiny ball. Tomorrow she would decide how best to deal with Ross and all the bewildering changes in her life. She was simply too tired to do anything about it now. She closed her eyes, and with the iron determination she used to rule others, she willed herself into sleep and the sweetest of dreams.

The following morning she stood before her cheval glass, examining her reflection with a critical eye. Her hair was tucked ruthlessly under a starched cap, and she'd donned one of her plainest gowns of dark gray cambric unadorned by so much as a single ribbon or ruffle. There, she thought, giving a decisive nod. She looked like her old self once more. Looking at her, no one would ever guess that she'd exchanged a passionate kiss in the moonlight with a man she was coming to care for more than was particularly proper or even wise. Thinking of all she had to do, she walked into her study, only to come to a startled halt at the sight that greeted her.

"Good heavens!" she gasped, glancing about her in astonishment. "What is all this?"

"For you, my dear," Aunt Matilda said, beaming at her in delight. "And there are even more of them in the entryway and drawing room! Is it not wonderful?"

Addy gazed at the forest of flowers, the act of speech for once beyond her capabilities. Flowers of every color and variety bloomed about her, their clashing fragrances rising to perfume the air with potent scents. Roses, lilies, violets, and some flowers whose names she didn't even know had been crammed into a variety of containers, and they covered every inch of surface in the already crowded room. Addy reached out a trembling finger to stroke the petal of a golden daffodil.

"But—but who sent them?" she asked in a bewildered tone, struggling to accept the overwhelming number of blossoms. She'd only been sent flowers once before in her life, and that a pitiful nosegay of indifferent wild-flowers sent to her by a former student in thanks for her assistance.

"Everyone!" her aunt exclaimed, gesturing at the mountain of cards on the table before her. "The pink roses are from Colonel Adamsleigh, and the lilies are from a Captain Davidson. The vulgar display of white and yellow roses are from Prinny, naturally, for the man does possess the most *appalling* taste, and the vase of pinks are from Major Kelmston. He also included a note asking if you would like to ride with him in the park later today. I sent a note accepting on your behalf."

"But I don't have a horse," Addy protested, lowering herself onto her chair in dazed shock. She shook her head and made a concentrated effort to regain control of her senses.

"Aunt, I don't understand," she said, glancing up to meet the older woman's gaze. "Why would all these men send me flowers? I have done nothing . . ."

"Nothing but to show yourself a brave and resource-ful young lady who has risen gallantly to their friend's defense," her aunt said, and then smirked at Addy's scowl. "And you needn't cast daggers at me, child, for I was but quoting from one of the cards. It came with the vase of gladiolus, if memory serves."

"Then it is because of Ross—Lord St. Jerome," Addy said, a feeling of relief stealing over her. It would be all right, she thought, if the flowers were thanks offered on Ross's behalf.

"No, Adalaide." Her aunt shook her head gently. " It is because of *you*. The flowers are for *you,* to thank *you.* They are your due, and you've only to accept and enjoy them."

Addy was annoyed to find tears pricking her eyes. Her aunt might think the stunning tribute had naught to do with Ross, but she knew better. The flowers were an indication of the esteem with which he was held by Society, an esteem she felt had long been owed to the man who had sacrificed so much for a world that had treated him so cruelly.

While she was coming to terms with her varying emotions, a footman came in bearing yet another floral tribute. Aunt Matilda was quick to snatch it up, the eager smile on her lips giving way to a smirk as she glanced at Addy.

"Speaking of his lordship," she said, offering the flowers and the card accompanying them to Addy. "For you, my dear."

Addy accepted the flowers curiously. Compared to the other flowers, the small bouquet of irises, placed in a delicate vase decorated with exquisitely painted thistles, was not much to speak of, but her breath caught in appreciation of its uncomplicated beauty. With hands that weren't quite steady, she unfolded the note and read:

My dear Miss Terrington,
   These flowers are not so blue as your eyes, nor does their perfume compare with the sweetness of your smile, but I fear they shall have to do. I pray you will accept them in thanks for all that you have done.

It was signed simply. *Ross.*

"Oh, how beautiful," Addy sighed, her eyes glowing as she raised the flowers to her nose to inhale the spicy fragrance. "Have you ever seen anything so lovely, Aunt Matilda?"

Her aunt studied her in satisfaction for several seconds before replying. "No, child, I cannot say that I have," she said smugly.

There was no time to linger over the flowers, as a flood of visitors poured into the house. Addy spent the next several hours dispensing tea and entertaining the men who had come to pay her court. Naturally, the large number of men guaranteed an equal number of ladies would also call, and Addy was forced to send to the pastry shop to make sure all of her guests were properly fed. Finally, she and her aunt were alone, and she collapsed against the settee, her eyes closing in weariness.

"I vow, if one more person comes through that door, I shall have them shot," Addy said with a disgruntled sigh. "Arm the servants, Aunt. Enough is enough."

" 'Tis too late to post sentries, Miss Terrington," Lord St. Jerome drawled from the doorway, his green eyes bright with laughter as he studied her. "The enemy has already landed."

Addy's eyes opened at his voice, aware of a heavy warmth spreading through her at the sight of him. As if it possessed a will of its own, her gaze fixed itself on his mouth, and she found herself remembering the strength and wonder of his kiss.

"Good day, my lord," she said, pulling her dignity about her as she sat up straight. "I am delighted to see you again. Thank you for the flowers. They are lovely."

He glanced about the room, his expression darkening as he took note of the other flowers. " 'Twould seem the thought was not as original as I had thought," he said with a low growl. "Who sent these, if I may ask?"

"Oh, everyone," Addy said blithely. She possessed enough feminine pride to gloat over his obvious disapproval. "There are more in the dining room and in my study as well, if you would care to see them," she added, offering him a polite smile.

His expression grew even blacker. "No, I thank you," he said, settling onto the chair nearest her. "I realize this is rather irregular, Miss Terrington," he began, his tone coldly formal as he met her gaze, "but might I have a word with you in private? I thought we might go for a walk, or a ride, if you would prefer. There are some things I should like to discuss with you."

Addy hesitated. Her first inclination was to accept, for she rather relished the notion of being private with him. On the other hand it was, as he said, highly irregular, and she didn't want him to think she was lost to all propriety. She threaded her fingers together, her brows knitting as she tried to decide how to best reason out this conundrum.

"I am afraid that won't be possible, my lord." Her aunt spoke first, giving Ross a regretful smile. "She has already promised Major Kelmston she would ride out with him, and it is past time she was getting ready."

"Go on, child," she added when Addy gaped at her in confusion. "I will see his lordship safely out. Off with you, now. Shoo." She waved her hand in obvious dismissal.

Aware she was being shamelessly maneuvered but uncertain what she should do about it, Addy had no choice but to follow her aunt's orders. "Very well, my lady," she said, her use of her aunt's rank subtly letting her aunt know of her displeasure. She also glanced at Ross, a genuine smile of regret on her lips as she offered him her hand.

"Perhaps we might walk in the park tomorrow, my lord," she said, heart thundering as he rose to tower over her.

"Aye," he agreed, his tanned fingers curving strongly about hers as he raised her hand to his lips. "Perhaps we might." He bent his head, but instead of kissing the back of her hand as she expected, he turned her hand over. Holding her gaze with his own, he touched his lips to her wrist.

"Ride well, *annsachd,*" he told her in a husky voice. "Pray give the major my best wishes. Tell him as well 'twould be a pity for him to have survived Coruña, only to fall in Hyde Park."

Addy bent a suspicious look upon him. "What is that supposed to mean?" she demanded.

He merely smiled, his green eyes full of masculine smugness. "Tell him, *annsachd.* He will know what it means."

"He said that, did he?" Major Anthony Kelmston chuckled, light gray eyes bright with laughter as he grinned at Addy. "Aye, it sounds like the sergeant, true enough. Arrogant, decisive, and deadly."

"But what is he referring to?" Addy pressed, intrigued at the way he had summed up Ross's complex nature in a few pithy words.

The major glanced away, his handsome face taking on

a distant look. "He refers to the retreat, Miss Ter-rington," he said, his deep voice reflective. "I was a lowly lieutenant then, with scarce the wits to wipe my own . . . nose. I was ordered to provide cover for the withdrawal of the Artillery, and almost got myself and the men under my command slaughtered instead. We'd been left for dead, and would doubtlessly have achieved that state had the sergeant not happened along to save our hides. You might say I owe him my life, and a great many other things as well."

Addy bit her lip and looked across the rolling green expanse of lawn toward the elegant waters of the Serpen-tine. She'd read of the dangerous and desperate retreat across Portugal, and of the thousands of men who did not survive the journey, but until now she hadn't known Ross had been there.

"I see," she said softly. "But what about his remark about your falling here in the park? Not planning on coming up a cropper, are you?" She'd made a light stab at humor, and was rewarded by another low chuckle from the major.

"Not unless the sergeant makes good his threat and shoots me from my horse. And he could do it too, make no mistake," he added when Addy gave a strangled gasp. "All members of the Rifles are excellent shots, but Ser-geant MacCailan was a legend amongst legends. Was it necessary to make a gentleman of him, ma'am? We stand in sore need of him over the next months."

Addy knew he was referring to recent developments in Spain, and to the huge battle everyone said was but a few weeks away. The major had already mentioned he would be rejoining his regiment by week's end, and she knew several of the others would be sailing away as well. Sailing off to war, she thought, shivering delicately; off to their deaths, many of them. Would Ross sail away as well once he had done what Wellington wanted?

"Miss Terrington?" The major had leaned forward to lightly touch her gloved hand. "Are you all right, ma'am?" he asked, his light brown eyebrows meeting in a worried frown.

She tightened her hands around her reins, causing her placid mount to give a snort of annoyance. "I am fine, sir," she lied, scraping up a smile for his benefit. "My horse seems rather restive, and I fear I am a poor horsewoman at best."

"I haven't given offense, have I?" the major asked, showing the keen sense of awareness Ross often displayed. "I was only teasing you, you know. Adamsleigh confided to me you are acting at the general's behest, and we are all of us more grateful than you may know. It will be a disaster if Wellington is recalled, ma'am. A disaster. Anything you can do to prevent that from happening will place all of England in your debt."

Addy didn't know what to say. The notion of having an entire nation indebted to her was more than a trifle disconcerting. It strengthened her resolve, making it even more imperative that she not fail. They rode along in companionable silence for several seconds before she spoke again.

"Major Kelmston, might I ask you a question?"

"Of course, Miss Terrington. What is it?"

"Colonel Adamsleigh mentioned he was bringing Lord St. Jerome a commission," she said, trying to keep the fear that was clawing at her out of her voice. "Does this mean his lordship is still in the Army? It was my understanding he was cashiered out when he came into his uncle's title. Or is the promotion an honorary one?" she added, a sudden hope stirring within her breast.

"In a manner of speaking, I suppose you might say that," he agreed, his tone reflective. "St. Jerome is now a captain, although he at present has no company to command. But I daresay that shouldn't be much of a problem for him, eh?" he said, grinning engagingly at Addy. "With all the gold at his command, he could buy an entire regiment and the colonel's eagle to go with it if he was of a mind. And if I know the sergeant—captain, that is—that is precisely what he will do. The man is a soldier through and through."

Addy's heart twisted painfully in her chest before plummeting to her toes. "Yes," she agreed, her shoulders slumping in defeat. "He is that."

"I am not certain I take your meaning, Lady Fareham," Ross said, his voice carefully controlled as he faced the older woman across the tea table. "What do you mean Adalaide's future is in my hands?" He and the tart-tongued widow were sitting in the study, where she'd dragged him shortly after Addy had ridden off with that young fool, Anthony Kelmston. The lad was well enough, Ross supposed, but that didn't mean he approved of him and Adalaide riding off without so much as a maid to accompany them.

"Come, sir," Lady Fareham said with a loud sniff, "you are a man of the world, and I am a lady in my dotage. If the pair of us cannot contrive to outwit the dear gel, all for her own good, mind, then of what use are we?"

Ross shifted uneasily in his chair. All this talk of marriage in relation to Adalaide was making him decidedly uneasy. He wondered if Lady Fareham had seen him and her niece out in the garden, and this was her way of reminding him of his duty. If so, he considered her point well taken, but that didn't mean he intended surrendering without first mounting a proper defense. He folded his arms across his chest and sent her a challenging scowl.

"But if Adalaide has chosen to remain unwed, then who are we to gainsay her?" he asked coolly. " 'Tis her life, is it not?"

Lady Fareham shook a gnarled finger at him. "Don't be anymore foolish than you can help being, young man," she said sharply. "No lady with half a brain in her head *wants* to be married, but what other choice has she? It's the way of the world, I am sad to say, and there is not a blessed thing we can do about it. If Adalaide is to have the smallest chance of happiness in this life, it is as a married lady. You say you owe her much, and so you do. All I am asking is that you repay that debt. Are you going to do this, or are you not?"

With that put so bluntly before him, Ross accepted there was nothing he could do. "Are you saying you wish me to marry your niece in order to repay my debt to her?" he demanded. If he was to be dragooned into marriage, he wanted it understood he knew that was precisely what was going on.

"Of course not! I certainly said no such thing!"

Ross shook his head, certain his hearing had played him false. "But my lady, you said—"

"Men are such singularly thickheaded creatures," Lady Fareham opined, mimicking his stance by folding her arms across her chest and meeting him scowl for scowl. " 'Tis no small wonder to me you are always making wars upon one another. You haven' t an ounce of common sense among you."

Ross clenched his jaw so hard, 'twas a wonder to him it did not snap. "I beg your pardon, madam, but I—"

"What I *said,* young man," she continued, "and what I expect you to do, is to help Adalaide find herself a husband amongst the fine young men she has flitting about her. You know most of them, do you not? Simply chose one, and leave the rest to me. Really, it is the simplest thing in the world! I cannot see why you insist upon making a Cheltenham tragedy out of it all."

"You want me to choose Adalaide a husband?" Ross was on his feet, staring down at her in shock. The woman was mad, he decided. No wonder Adalaide could be so strong-headed at times. Her family had left the rearing of her to a Bedlamite.

"Indeed I do," Lady Fareham said, nodding approvingly. "You see? It is not so difficult to understand once you approach the matter logically."

"Logically!" The word burst from his lips in a frustrated growl. "I doubt, my lady, if you even know the meaning of the word! And I thought Adalaide the most stubborn and willful female on the face of this earth." He threw himself back on to his seat with a muttered imprecation in Gaelic. If he thought to give offense, 'twas plain he had underestimated his hostess. The older lady fair preened at his words.

"Of course, it is how I taught her to be. Although"—

she frowned—"I fear 'tis a lesson the dear child has learned all too well. Convincing her to change her mind will be no easy task. But never fear, my lord," she said, offering Ross a bright smile. "I am sure you are more than equal to the task."

Ross stared at the older lady in sudden suspicion. "What sort of rig are you running, Ma'am?"

"None whatsoever, my lord," Lady Fareham assured him with a serene look. "Now finish your tea. Adalaide will soon be returning, and we've much to accomplish before she does. Why are you looking at me like that?" she added, as Ross continued studying her with hard-eyed scrutiny.

"I was wondering, ma'am, why we men are so foolish as to leave you ladies out of the Army, when if we left the running of the war to you, you would have all accomplished within a fortnight." He picked up the tea he had discarded earlier and took a thoughtful sip. "Doubtlessly 'tis because we are the slow-witted, thickheaded creatures that you name us," he added, flashing her a companionable smile.

Lady Fareham tilted her head to one side. "Yes," she said, smiling approvingly in return. "That is what it must be."

They continued chatting, and Ross felt himself warming to the older woman. This would be Adalaide in a few decades, he mused, feeling an odd pang at the thought he'd not be there to see it. Thinking of that made him think of something else, and he slanted her a curious look.

"Now what is it, lad?" she asked with an impatient sigh. "I vow, you are the most annoying man, always staring at a person as if you would know their innermost secrets."

He smiled. When he'd been a sergeant, such conduct had been called presumptuous, and had usually earned him a quick backhand across the face. Now 'twas an annoying habit.

"I was trying to remember, my lady, if Adalaide ever mentioned your precise rank to me," he said, for it was more or less the truth. "I know you are widowed and stand as her chaperon, but that is all I know of you."

"Oh, is that all?" Her shoulders shifted in an indifferent shrug. "Well, 'tis no great mystery, I can tell you that much. I was married at the age of seventeen to the Earl of Fareham, a gentleman three times my age. He needed an heir, you see, and decided I would do quite nicely. We were wed eleven years, and in all that time I bore five babes, all of whom died within a few days. He was quite put out, convinced he'd made a bad bargain, and had me sent away. He died some fourteen years later, and I never saw him again. A distant cousin inherited the title, I believe, and he sent me a small stipend to make certain I wouldn't lay a claim against the estate."

Ross wasn't certain what he should say. There wasn't a trace of emotion in the older lady's voice; merely a simple recitation of the facts. Yet he felt as if he should say something. He studied her lined face and her proud, tired eyes before speaking.

"I am sorry, my lady, for the babes you lost," he said in a soft voice. "It must have been hard."

Her teacup rattled in her hand. "It was hell," she said quietly. "But when Adalaide came to live with me, it was almost like having a daughter of my own. That is why I am so determined she should marry, and well. A woman alone is a woman without power, and I don't want that for her."

It occurred to Ross he had been presented the perfect opportunity to repay both ladies for the kindness they had shown him. He had to marry someone, he told himself. Why should it not be Adalaide? She was a lady, was she not? And thanks to his uncle's gold, her lack of a dowry would prove no great matter. There was the matter of her sharp tongue and willful ways to be considered, but he'd grown rather fond of both in the past weeks, and so he could dismiss them as well.

Then there was the physical side of marriage, he thought, smiling in memory of the single kiss they had shared. He'd never known such pain and such pleasure, and the idea of having her in his bed was a temptation too sweet to resist. Yes, he decided, his pulses racing with the heady anticipation he usually felt before a battle, he would do it. He would marry Adalaide. All that remained now was convincing his intended bride she wanted to marry him. A difficult task to be certain, but as he'd already told Adalaide, he was accustomed to fighting for what he wanted. He would wait until the vote to insure that Wellington remained in command was secured, and then he would begin a campaign of his own. A campaign that promised the sweetest of all possible rewards to the victor.

Ten

Addy was kept busy over the next few days. Mornings were given over to strategy sessions with Ross, and she was secretly delighted that he'd once more become a fixture in their house. Despite his preoccupation with the vote he always had some teasing words to offer her, usually about the beaus she seemed to have acquired, and he could always make her laugh at most of them. The rumors of his cowardice vanished as if they had never been, and the prince himself was the one to bestow his captaincy upon him. An honor that would have been the greater, Ross confided to her later, if he'd had the troops to match the pretty silver cord on his new jacket.

Her afternoons were given over to tutoring Lord Hixworth, although he was rapidly progressing to the stage where such instruction would no longer be required. He'd thrown himself into the battle for Wellington, and he grew more confident and certain of himself with each passing day. Who might have guessed politics was the shy young man's natural milieu, Addy mused, feeling an almost maternal pride as she listened to him practicing his maiden speech. She knew Ross was also set to make his first speech within a few weeks, but so far he hadn't shown it to her. She tried not to let it bother her, but it did.

At her aunt's urging, she'd also started instructing Mr. Wellford. Since he was more experienced with Society than most of her pupils, she was able to eschew her usual lessons. Her scheme to introduce him to several intellectual societies had proven more successful than she'd dared hope, and he opened up as he was able to associate with those who shared his many interests. He was even talking of her dear friend, Miss Elizabeth Morton, in the most glowing of terms, an affection that Elizabeth shyly admitted was more than returned.

Addy's nights were spent in the social round, and for reasons she still could not fully comprehend, she seemed to have "taken." Indeed, so great was her success with the gentlemen that Lady Sefton, the kindest of all the Patronesses at Almack's, took her aside and sweetly explained that they could no longer condone her wearing turbans and what her ladyship delicately called her "mourning clothes."

"For it confuses people, you see, to see such a lovely and fashionable young lady in half mourning," she said, patting Addy's hand. "They wonder who in your family might have died, and then wonder if they had ought to send flowers. Some color in your wardrobe, Miss Terrington, if you please."

"At least she didn't ask me to don white or sprigged muslin," Addy commented to Aunt Matilda as they made their way to yet another ball. "That would have been too lowering by half."

"I am not so certain of that," her aunt replied, toying

with the fringe of her shawl. "White would have been just the thing to show your hair to its best advantage. I daresay the world must have thought you bald as Good Queen Bess the way you insisted upon wearing those dreadful turbans."

"Perhaps, but I'm still not rigging myself out like a bride," Addy said decisively. "The Patronesses might have dusted me off and taken me from the shelf, but as far as I am concerned nothing has changed. I am determined to remain a spinster."

"If you say so, dearest."

Her aunt's placid acquiescence had Addy's eyes narrowing in sudden suspicion. "I am in earnest, ma'am," she felt compelled to warn the other woman. "I know this sudden popularity I seem to be enjoying has you thinking I have changed my mind, but I have not. I am not on the catch for a husband."

"I know you're not." Her aunt gave her a vague smile. "You're far too old for such nonsense. And so I told the viscount when he mentioned the matter to me yesterday."

"It is not that I have anything against the married state, per se," Addy continued resolutely. "It is just that I—" She stopped. "Ross mentioned marriage to you yesterday?"

"Not in so many words," her aunt replied, sounding bored. "He merely mentioned that he wondered if you meant to marry one of the charming young men buzzing about you, and I assured him you did not.

"He is quite fond of you, you know," she added with a chuckle. "I think he sees himself as a surrogate brother to you, and thinks it his duty to keep a sharp eye on you.

Heaven knows Arthur and Reginald would hand you over to the first young man to ask for your hand, and as for Richard, well, the less said of *that* particular individual, the better."

Addy grimaced at the mention of her eldest brother. He avoided London at all costs, declaring it no fit place for a Christian gentleman, and was always after her to return to the country. He was married to the only daughter of a nearby squire, a match Addy herself had helped make possible when she'd managed to make her priggish and countrified brother into something passing in the provinces for a London gentleman.

She'd done the same for all her brothers and several male cousins, which was how she'd achieved her current reputation. But instead of being grateful, Richard had turned into a sanctimonious tyrant, fond of giving lectures and firing off missives on a weekly basis. The last one contained a strongly worded hint that she stop "dithering about," as he termed it, and marry one of the men dangling after her before "they come to their senses and turn their attentions elsewhere."

"I do not see why his lordship should see the need to stand as my brother," she complained, responding belatedly to her aunt's teasing comments. *"I* do not see myself as his sister."

Her aunt smiled. "I know."

Addy would have pursued that remark, but they were already pulling up in front of the home of Lord Grayburgh. His lordship was hosting a ball to honor several officers who were about to depart London for Spain, but all knew the real reason was a show of support for Wellington. It was nearing the last week of June, and the vote could no longer be postponed.

Inside, she was quickly swept away by her crowd of admirers, and she spent the next hour dancing and talking to her many new friends. But no matter how busy she was, she was always aware Ross was nearby. He was leading a pretty blonde out to dance when she was joining a set, or flirting with a sultry brunette while she was accepting a cup of punch one of her suitors offered her. Always there, she realized, always just out of reach.

There was to be more dancing following a light supper, and Addy was sitting beside her aunt waiting for her next partner to claim her. But instead of the dashing Naval officer she was expecting, it was Ross who was bowing over her hand.

"My dance, I believe, Miss Terrington," he said, his eyes gleaming with admiration as they swept over her.

Addy's heart leapt into her throat before she forced it back down to its proper location. "I'm afraid you are mistaken, my lord," she said with genuine regret. "This dance is promised to Lieutenant Grisby." She attempted to free her hand, only to have his fingers tighten about her own.

"Unfortunately, the lieutenant has been unavoidably detained," he said, drawing her to her feet. "He has asked me to serve in his stead. Shall we go? The set is forming."

Short of making a scene and drawing even more interested gazes to their corner, Addy had no choice but to allow him to lead her out onto the dance floor. They were halfway through the set when something made her glance toward the door. A crowd of young Army officers had Lieutenant Grisby surrounded, and it was obvious from the frustrated expression on his face it was not a situation he found to his liking. Understanding dawned, and she flashed Ross a reproving look.

"An interesting maneuver, sir," she admonished, albeit with lips curved in an appreciative smile. "It must be the first time in history the Cavalry has bottled up the Navy."

He didn't bother denying the charge. "I'll have to mention it to the general when next we meet," he said, flashing the lieutenant a victorious look. " 'Tis not without its risks, I grant you, but then"—he glanced back down at her—" 'tis not without its rewards."

Before she could respond, he was leading her back to her aunt. After offering each of them a polite bow, he disappeared into the crowd, only to reappear just as the party was ending. He walked up behind her in the entry-way, slipping her velvet cape about her in a gesture that was oddly proprietary.

"I've told your aunt I would see you home," he said, his hands lingering briefly on her shoulders. "There are some things I would discuss with you."

That sounded ominous, but Addy kept her expression carefully blank as he led her out to his waiting carriage. She paused at the sight of the three hulking men stand-ing beside it. Though they were all dressed in livery, she'd never seen three rougher or more deadly-looking men in her life.

"Captain!" The largest of the men shot to attention, firing off a brisk salute before opening the carriage door. "Perimeter is secured, sir, and no sign of the enemy has been spotted."

Ross returned the salute as if it were the most natural thing in the world. "Thank you, Malton," he said calmly. "You and the others may assume your positions. Tell Shorts he is to take the route around the park before taking us to Bruton Street."

"Aye, sir!" Another salute was snapped off, and then Malton was helping Addy into the coach with more enthusiasm than skill. The moment the door had closed behind them she turned to Ross.

"Well, sir?" she asked, her brow raised in inquiry. "I am waiting for an explanation. Your staff is most . . . interesting."

He gave a negligent shrug. "London is full of cashiered soldiers in need of work. I give it to them."

"And that business about 'the enemy'?" she pressed, touched by his concern for the men he'd once fought with. "Do you really expect your cousin to do something untoward?"

"There is no crime I'd not think that sot capable of," he responded with a low grumble. "But no, I do not expect him to be so bold as to make an outright move against me."

"Then why the guards?"

"Devil take it, woman, the men have their pride!" he exclaimed, glaring at her in frustration. "Would you have that taken from them along with everything else? Giving them coin for their pockets and food for their bellies is not enough. A man needs purpose as well, and so I give it to them."

"Guarding you from an attack you don't really expect?"

"Who is to say what that gutless worm may do?" he

retorted, hunching his shoulders and folding his arms across his chest. "This way 'tis employment I am offering them, and not charity. Charity sticks in a man's throat, however empty his stomach, but honest work is another matter. I hire them on as guards until I am able to find them other positions."

Addy's throat tightened painfully. She knew Ross too well to praise him for his largesse. He would only scowl and say 'twas nothing and then change the subject, but she doubted if the men in his employ would dismiss his kindness so easily. He'd saved them, she thought, and in saving them, perhaps he was in some way saving himself. It was an interesting notion.

They rode along in silence for several minutes, and Addy took the opportunity to study him at her leisure. For a man who insisted he had something important to discuss with her, Ross was oddly silent. His dark gold brows were set in a straight line over his hooded eyes, and his full, sensual mouth was thinned in obvious displeasure. He was clearly angry about something, and she wondered if he was about to issue her a lecture about some failing of hers. The man was near as fond of lectures as was Richard, and Addy knew she wasn't up to being on the receiving end of such a scold. Without giving herself time to reconsider, she joined him on his side of the coach.

"Ross?" She touched his cheek with a gentle hand. "What is wrong? Are you angry with me?"

He turned his head at that, his eyes meeting hers with a fierceness that had the breath catching in her throat. It wasn't impatience or disapproval she saw shimmering in the rich green depths of his eyes. It was desire; desire for her. She was still absorbing the shock of that when his hand stole up to touch her as she was touching him.

"How can I be angry with you, *leannan?*" he asked in a voice made husky with passion. "When I want you so much I am mad with the wanting?"

Addy's pulses began their wild racing, and her breath seemed clogged in her lungs. Sitting so close to Ross, she could feel the tension holding his muscular body taut, and the knowledge that he was waiting for her decision had her senses swimming with an intoxicating brew of emotions. She knew she had but to move back, and that would be the end of it. What came next would be at her choice, and looking into his compelling eyes, she knew what that choice would be.

"I am glad you want you me, Ross," she said, feeling like the greatest hussy in London and reveling in the sensation. "I am glad, because I want you as well."

His eyes flared with a burst of satisfaction, and then he was sweeping her into his arms, his mouth hot and fiercely demanding as it covered hers. The kiss was every bit as wondrous and as stirring as the first they had shared, and Addy's head spun with delight. Ross's mouth was ardent in its demand, moving skillfully against hers until she parted her lips in shy acquiescence. Immediately his tongue surged between her lips, flicking against her own until she was breathless with a wild passion.

"Ross." She moaned his name when he freed her mouth to brush a searing kiss down her neck. "Kiss me, please kiss me!"

His mouth took hers again, harder and even more demanding, seeking a response she was only too happy to give him. This was the passion she had always wanted, the passion she was so certain she would never know. Now that she'd found it, she wanted never to let it go. They continued kissing, their lips never seeming to tire of the taste and texture of one another. She knew her actions put her beyond the pale, but she didn't care. When she felt Ross's fingers gently brushing over her breasts, she gave a soft cry of delight.

"You are sweet, so soft," he groaned, his fingertips caressing the turgid peak of her breast. "How you make me burn, *annsachd,* like a fire on the coldest days."

Addy's arms stole tighter about his neck, pressing him closer to her trembling body. He complied eagerly, and when his lips sought her breasts, she bit her lips to hold back her groan.

Without warning the carriage gave a rough jolt, and the violent movement almost sent Addy flying to the floor.

"Bleedin' idiot!" a rough voice called out. "Learn 'ow to drives why don't yer, ye ham-handed chaw bacon!"

Ross helped steady her, although his own hands shook with visible tremors. "Are you all right?" he asked, his tone harsh. "You were not injured?"

"N-no, I am fine," Addy stammered, understanding with regret that the sensual interlude was at an end. She knew she should be grateful, but it was rather hard to be grateful when her entire body was throbbing with a wild, burning ache. Taking a deep breath, she managed to gather enough courage to meet his gaze.

"I suppose I should apologize," she began, feeling awkward. "I don't make a habit of forgetting myself with gentlemen in carriages, I assure you."

The mouth that had been devouring hers only moments before tightened in displeasure. "I did not think you did," he said, his voice as cold and distant as his expression. "We will speak no more of it."

She flinched, cut to the quick by his sudden withdrawal. Tears threatened, but she would not allow them to fall. She moved quickly back to her own seat, gathering her cloak and the tattered remnants of her pride about her.

"You said you wanted to speak with me, Lord St. Jerome," she said, resisting the urge to straighten the spectacles that were sitting crookedly on her face. "What is it you wished to say?"

He studied her for a few moments before responding. "Nothing that cannot wait, Miss Terrington," he said, mimicking her stilted voice. "I will call upon you tomorrow."

Addy's jaw tensed at his arrogant assumption she should be at his beck and call. If he thought he could kiss her senseless one moment and then cut her dead in the next, he was about to learn such was not the case. She raised her chin and gave him the look she usually reserved for overly presumptuous clerks.

"That will not be possible, my lord," she said, taking grim satisfaction in the anger that flared to life in his eyes. "I fear I will not be available."

He leaned forward and she jerked back, thinking he was about to shake her. Instead he straightened her spectacles, making certain they were correctly positioned on the bridge of her nose before leaning back against the seat.

"Be available, *leannan*," he advised, his eyes soft with

menace as he crossed his arms. "Be available, or I fear I shall have to do something we will both have cause to regret."

Fool! *Baothalan!* Ross cursed himself in English and Gaelic as the coach rumbled its way back to Berkeley Square. He'd meant to cautiously broach the subject of marriage with Adalaide, and what did he do the moment they were alone but pounce upon her like a wolf upon a particularly tasty lamb. And afterwards, what had he done but compounded his sin by turning proper as a bishop at tea. No wonder she'd refused to see him, he thought, grinding his teeth in frustration. He would count himself luckier than he deserved if the little *deamhan* ever spoke to him again.

He was still cursing himself the following morning when he went into his study and found Nevil waiting to speak with him.

"Good morning, my lord," the other man said, bowing formally. "I trust you are well?"

"The plague take you, Nevil," he snarled, throwing himself onto the chair behind his desk and propping his booted feet on the desk's glossy surface. "I told you never to call me that when we are private. And if you bow at me again, I'll kick your arse up between your ears!"

Instead of taking offense, the other man roared with laughter. "Aye, Captain . . . or do you prefer I call you Sergeant?" He sent Ross a cheeky wink. "I prefer my arse remains where it is"

Ross's lips quirked in a reluctant smile. "Captain will

do," he said, his black temper dissipating somewhat. "Now, tell me why you have decided to honor me with your presence. Have you found some other soldiers in need of employment?"

"Oh, there's always men in want of work, Captain," Nevil said, scratching his jaw. "But that's not why I'm here. Your cousin was seen at the moneylenders yesterday evening. Have a care, sir. A cornered enemy is a dangerous enemy."

"Aye, Corporal, I know," he said evenly. What he didn't say as well was that he knew all about Atherton's visit to the moneylenders. With Falconer's help he had been buying up his cousin's vowels, and was using them to pressure him into silence. This rumor had been easily dispelled. They might not be so fortunate the next time.

"I've two men watching him," Nevil continued, lowering himself onto one of the chairs facing the desk. "Shall I hire on more?"

Ross thought of the men Nevil mentioned in want of work. "No," he said, "but I want you to hire on some men to watch Miss Terrington and her aunt. My cousin bears her as great a hatred as he does me, and it would be just like the gutless *cacc* to attack her rather than me."

"Aye, Captain. Any further instructions?"

"No, that should be it for the moment," Ross said, then turned his attention to another problem that was troubling him. "What news have you from Spain?" he asked, knowing the cashiered soldier visited the docks daily and would best know the latest intelligence.

Nevil did not disappoint him. "Rumor is they've cornered the whole of the French Army near the frontier.

King Joseph is said to be with them, and carrying half his household with him. Jourdan is in a rare fit, for he'd have his troops halfway to Paris if the emperor's brother didn't have him so bogged down. Can you imagine the riches to be had if we are victorious?" He gave a wistful sigh.

Ross said nothing. Looting was as much a part of a battle as killing, and although he'd never stooped to picking a fallen enemy's pockets, he could understand why others were not so nice in their notions. A man with nothing save the clothes on his back would be hard-pressed to pass by a fortune.

"What of the French artillery?" he asked, knowing they posed the greatest threat to the British line. Say what one would about Jourdan, the dandified French general knew how to make deadly use of his cannon.

"Interspersed with the other wagons. I spoke with a lad who was in Spain but a week past, and he says that Wellington has the road to Madrid completely blocked. The battle will come within a few days' time, if it has not already been fought."

Ross's lips tightened, and he found himself wishing he was back in Spain. The troops would be trapped in that odd state between fear and excitement, and they would need calming. As a sergeant he'd spent most of his time before a battle moving amongst the men, soothing them, and making sure they were as prepared as could be for what would come. Much good he would do anyone here, he thought, his lips twisting with bitterness.

Later, at his club, all the talk was of the battles. The one brewing in Spain, and the one reaching the boiling point in Parliament.

"Hope you've your speech ready, lad." The Duke of Creshton slapped a friendly hand on Ross's back. "You'll be giving it in two hours' time."

Ross felt himself blanch. "Today?" he asked, his mind going blank with fear. "But your grace, I—I had other plans for today. I was going to ask Miss Terrington to be my wife."

"Have to wait, won't it?" the older man said, winking. "Just mind you don't wait too long, eh? You've a bit of competition there. Is that not so, Falconer?" He glanced at the marquess, who was sitting coolly sipping his brandy.

"More than a bit, your grace," Falconer answered in his calm tones. "But I am certain his lordship will prove himself the victor."

The duke roared at that. "To be sure, Falconer, to be sure. Well, lads, I'm off to Parliament. Mind you come straight there, St. Jerome, and you as well, Falconer. If all goes as we hope, we'll have much to celebrate to-night."

After he'd taken his leave, Ross turned a worried look on the marquess. "Will it go as he says?" he asked, frowning. "I find it hard to believe victory will be as easily won as that."

In answer Falconer gave a careless shrug. "Did you not read *The Times* this morning? The paper was full of the coming battle, and equally full of praise for Wellington. A vote to remove him now would cause rioting in the streets, and give considerable comfort to the French. Not even the earl's bitterest foes would dare risk such a thing."

Ross contemplated that for a moment. "Then perhaps," he began, feeling like the greatest coward alive, "it won't be necessary that I address the House. If the vote is assured . . ."

Falconer actually laughed, his gold-colored eyes brilliant with amusement. "No vote is assured, Captain, until after it has been counted. Do not let it worry you. No one ever listens to the speeches. Just mind the snoring doesn't drown you out."

Ross raised his glass in a mocking toast. "Thank you, my lord."

"You are welcome," Falconer returned, picking up his glass and taking another sip. "Now, tell me more of your plan to marry Miss Terrington. She is a lovely lady."

"Aye." Ross settled back in his chair, a warm glow of satisfaction spreading through him. "She is. She's a good head on her shoulders, when she's not in a temper about something, and she's not the silly sort of chit to expect undying vows of love or other romantic drivel. A calm, practical sort of wife she'll make." The thought had him beaming.

Falconer set his glass down with exaggerated care. "Is this the offer you mean to make her?"

"Aye," Ross repeated, frowning at the odd note in the marquess's voice. "A wee bit better phrased, of course, but essentially, that is what I will say. I've given the matter some thought and I've decided that if I must marry, then it should at least be to a lady I admire. Adalaide is such a lady, and once I've put the matter to her she'll agree soon enough. 'Twill be a good marriage," he added defensively, uncertain if it was the marquess he was trying to convince, or himself.

Falconer shook his head. "It is as well I didn't wager

with his grace," he said, addressing Ross sternly. "You're mad as can be if you think any female, even one as practical as Miss Terrington, would accept so insulting an offer."

"Insulting!" Ross roared at the word, then hastily lowered his voice when he realized he'd drawn the disapproving looks of the other members. "It's my name I'm offering her," he continued, taking care to keep his voice low-pitched. "And a fine title to go with it! *She* is the one who would be mad, to turn down the chance to be a lady. Stubborn and contrary I'll admit she is, but she has as sharp a mind as you could hope for. She'll see the sense of our marrying."

Falconer raised his eyes heavenward in an obvious plea for divine guidance. "I pray the speech you give in the general's defense is more persuasive than that, else Wellington is as good as recalled," he said, and then pointed a condemning finger at Ross.

"Females, St. Jerome," he said in the manner of a sergeant drilling a line of not overly bright recruits, "are far more interested in sentiment than sense. Never mind their talk of logic and reason. When it comes to the matter of matrimony, it's words of love and endless passion they're wanting, not a bunch of prattle about admiration and duty. And the more intellectual a lady pretends to be, the more romantic her soul. I vow, if you scratch half the so-called bluestockings in London, they will bleed prose straight from a Minervian novel. Hypocrites, the whole bloody lot of them."

Ross's eyebrows raised at the venom in the marquess's voice. "You sound as if you have some experience in this, my lord."

"I have," Falconer assured him resentfully, "and that is why I am telling you that if you are set to marry Miss Terrington, you'd best reconsider how you make your offer, else she will turn her pert nose up at you and tell you to go to the devil."

Ross had a sudden vision of Adalaide doing just that, accompanied, no doubt, by a lecture on the proper way to propose marriage to a lady. It would be just like her, he thought, running a distracted hand through his hair.

"Then what am I to do?" he asked, more of himself than Falconer, but it was Falconer who answered.

"Wait," he cautioned, setting down his glass and rising to his feet "No need to march into the cannon's mouth until it is absolutely necessary. In the meanwhile, Parliament awaits."

Eleven

Whether by happenstance or design, Addy found it necessary to spend the greater part of the day away from the house. First there were the books she simply *had* to return to the circulating library; then there were the courtesy calls she couldn't put off another day. And since she was actually dancing these days, a pair of dancing slippers necessitated visits to several shops as well as a brief stop at her modiste's to discuss a new gown.

As it happened, this was also the day her Scientific Society was set to meet. Even though she'd previously sent her regrets, Addy decided nothing would do but she attend and listen to Sir Humphrey Davies discuss his latest experiments. She'd settled into her seat and was chatting with one of her oldest friends when a commotion at the door made her glance up. To her amazement, Lord Hixworth was making straight for her, his face set in an expression of the sternest resolve.

"Miss Terrington," he greeted her with a curt bow. "I am glad to have tracked you to earth at last. We must leave at once, else we shall be too late."

Addy paled at these ominous words. "Has something

happened?" she asked, her fingers clenching about her reticule. "My aunt?"

"Eh?" The earl looked puzzled, and then shook his head. "Oh, no, Miss Terrington, I beg pardon. I hadn't meant to alarm you. Her ladyship is fine. It is Lord St. Jerome. We really must go, ma'am. My coach and team are waiting outside."

Addy needed no further urging. With more haste than grace she gathered up her gloves and reticule, her fingers trembling as fear and fury consumed her. It had to be that wretched cousin of his, she thought, fighting back a rising sense of despair. If the man had hurt Ross in any way, she would tear him to pieces.

There was an agonizing wait while a servant fetched her cloak and bonnet, and then they were hurrying down the steps and into the waiting carriage. The moment they were under way, she raised her chin and met the earl's somber gaze.

"What has happened?" she asked, steeling herself to hear the worst. "Tell me at once, else I shan't be able to endure it! Is his lordship badly injured?"

"Injured?" Hixworth blinked at her. "No, I shouldn't say he was injured. A bit shaken, perhaps, and looking as if he's ready to cast up his accounts, but resolved to his duty nonetheless."

It was to be a duel, then, Addy thought, blowing out the breath she had unconsciously been holding. It was still dangerous, and likely to make the scandal of the season. Perhaps she could talk him into merely wounding Atherton, she thought optimistically. However vicious and unprincipled he might be, no man deserved to die for such sins. If such was the case, half of Society would be lying dead on a field of honor.

"When is it to occur?" she asked, her practical nature rising to the fore. From what Hixworth said there was still time to act, and she was prepared to do whatever was required to make Ross see the error of his ways. They'd worked too hard for too long to risk losing it all.

"In less than an hour's time," Hixworth said, dragging out his watch and consulting it with a scowl. "Which is why we must make all possible haste. If we are much later, there will be no room for you in the Gallery."

Gallery? Addy shook her head as if to clear it. *"Where* is it to take place?" she asked, wondering if the earl had taken leave of his senses.

"The House of Lords, of course," Hixworth said, the look on his face making it plain he was thinking much the same thing of her. "Where else would he make his maiden speech?"

"His speech?" Addy exclaimed in indignation. "You dragged me from my meeting because Ross is going to make a speech?"

"Not just a speech, Miss Terrington," he corrected with a prim sniff. "His first speech as a member of the House of Lords, and what is more, the Duke of Creshton and the others have arranged for the vote to be taken directly afterward. Everything we have worked for will culminate in this afternoon. Naturally, I thought you would want to be present."

And so she would have, Addy thought, feeling a sharp prick of pain, if Ross had seen fit to invite her. But he hadn't, and that hurt more than she thought possible.

"Perhaps it would be best if I did not attend," she said, striving for what dignity she could muster.

The earl gaped at her in astonishment. "Do you mean you do not wish to?"

"No, of course not," she said, then hastily tried to explain. "That is to say, I *do* wish to attend, but I'm not at all certain Lord St. Jerome feels the same. If he did, wouldn't he have invited me himself?"

Hixworth's brow cleared as if by magic. "As to that, Miss Terrington, I know he fully intended doing so, but he didn't have the time. The general's friends decided to call for the vote now rather than later, and he didn't have time to get a message to you. But of course he would want you there. You are his friend, are you not?"

Yes, Addy decided with a depressed sigh, she supposed she was that. Or at least that was what she should be. It was certainly no fault of Ross's she had fallen in love with him. Such a thing was no one's fault. It was just—she stopped, the blood draining from her face as she realized the import of her thoughts.

In love, she realized dully, listening to the thunder of her own heart. With Ross. Dear heaven! She was in love with Ross! Like a rush of wind a thousand images flowed through her mind, and with them was a joy so great she thought she would die from it. She saw Ross as she had the first time she had seen him, unconscious, ill, and yet possessed of a power and a strength that had entranced her from the start. She saw his eyes flashing with temper, dancing with mischief, and bright with passion as he bent over her . . .

"Miss Terrington?" Lord Hixworth was looking at her askance. "We have reached Parliament. Do you wish to come in? If you do not, I can have the coachman drive you to your home."

Addy shook her head, forcing the sweet memories to the back of her mind. "I will come with you," she said decisively, gathering up her belongings. Her discovery was too new, and the enormity of it too frightening, for her to deal with it now. Later, when she was alone, she would decide what to do about her errant emotions. For now, she wanted to hear the man she loved make his speech and prove his true worth to all the world.

"And to conclude, my lords, I would put you in the boots of the common soldier. A man like myself, facing a line of Imperial troops waiting only for the chance to cut him and his fellows down. He has but one chance in a hundred, mayhap one chance in a thousand, to survive this day, and that chance is Wellington. Would you take that chance from him? From me? From your sons and brothers? I pray that you cannot. Thank you."

Ross collapsed on his chair, his knees shaking so violently 'twas a wonder to him they had managed to support him at all. It was over, God be praised, and he vowed never to put himself through such torment again. Fighting battles was child's play compared to speechmaking, and Ross wasn't ashamed to admit which he preferred.

A silence greeted his closing words, a silence that to Ross's ears seemed deafening in its enormity. Then someone started clapping, then another person, and another, and soon it seemed everyone was clapping, shouting as they surged to their feet.

"Bravo!"

"Well done!"

"Huzzah!"

"God save the Earl of Wellington!"

The shouts rang out, filling the staid and ancient chambers with a cacophony of sound. Around him the other members were clapping him on his back and shaking his hand, pledging him their support. The duke hurried over to pump his hand.

"Excellently done, lad! Superbly done! The vote is now ours, and 'tis all due to you!"

Ross accepted the praise and congratulations in numbed silence, unable to believe it was all over. He felt much the same in the aftermath of a battle, when against all odds he found himself still to be alive. He was usually exhausted, wearily grateful, and sickened at what he'd had to do to remain alive.

"Congratulations, Ross." Falconer stood before him, offering him his hand and a warm smile. "You have done your duty."

Ross accepted the other man's hand gratefully. "Thank you," he said. "But I am sure you will understand if I tell you I have no intention of giving another speech for as long as I live."

Falconer gave one of his rare laughs. "As with a great many other things in this life, speech-making grows easier with practice. The first time is always the most difficult. But you did well, sir; well indeed. And I am not the only one to think so." He indicated the large gallery located across the huge expanse of the room.

Ross glanced up, his jaw almost dropping when he saw it was filled to overflowing with people, all shouting and cheering. It was just as well he had not known they were there, he thought, swallowing uneasily. If he had, it was likely he wouldn't have been able to utter a single word. He had raised his hand to acknowledge the crowd when he saw a familiar face.

"Good Lord, is that Adalaide?" he demanded, straining his eyes for a better look. She was standing nearest the rail waving her handkerchief, and while he looked on in horror, she was shoved and buffeted by the surging crowd.

"She will be crushed!" he cried, forgetting everything but the danger to Adalaide. He started forward, only to stop when Falconer stepped in front of him.

"And if you go up there, you will likely be torn to bits by that overly enthusiastic mob," Falconer said, his voice making it plain he would brook no opposition. "Stay here. I will go and rescue your prospective bride."

Ross shook off the restraining hand, fury in his eyes. "I know you mean well," he said, his accent deepening with the force of his emotions. "But never put yourself between Adalaide and myself again. I'll no' be having it."

Other than raising his eyebrows, Falconer gave no outward sign of discomfiture. He simply stepped back, hands held at shoulder level, as Ross pushed his way past him and began making his way toward the balcony. It was a long, impossible journey, made all the more difficult by the fact that half the people in London seemed determined to talk to him. He kept moving, doing his best to keep a desperate eye on Adalaide. The crowd continued swirling around her, and she seemed impossibly tiny and defenseless. Suddenly the crowd surged from behind, and she stumbled, disappearing into the ocean of humanity.

"Adalaide!" Her name was torn from his anguished throat. He began to run, shoving aside anyone foolish enough to get in his way. He was halfway up the Visitors Staircase when he once more found his path blocked, this time by an ill-clothed behemoth of a man who stood grinning down at him with a wide, broken-toothed smile.

"Not to worry, Cap'n," the giant told Ross. "I've yer ladyship right here." He dragged forth a small, struggling bundle of outraged femininity.

"Let me go, you great bear of a bully!" Adalaide was swinging her rather battered-looking reticule at the man's arms. "How dare you accost a lady!"

"Adalaide." Ross was uncertain whether to laugh or cry. Her small plumed bonnet was sadly crushed, and her spectacles sat askew on her flushed face. When she heard his voice she turned and looked at him, her expression of indignation giving way to one of relief.

"Ross, you must have this ruffian taken up at once!" she said, pulling desperately to free her arm. "A fine world we have when an unprotected female cannot listen to a political speech without being inopportuned!"

"I will look into the matter for you, my dear," he managed, fighting the ridiculous urge to laugh. Here he'd been terrified Adalaide was in danger of being crushed, and when he finally found her, she was dressing down a man nearly twice her size.

"I have her now, sir, I thank you," Ross said, holding his hand out to the other man. "I assume you are one of the soldiers hired by Corporal Collier to follow Miss Terrington?"

"Aye, Cap'n." The giant saluted, nearly felling several passersby who were attempting to make their way around him. "George Barker, sir, at yer service!"

"My compliments, Mr. Barker," Ross replied, calmly reaching out and plucking Adalaide from the giant's grasp. "Do you like horses, Mr. Barker?"

"Horses, sir?" Mr. Barker scratched his lantern-size jaw and squinted in thought. "Aye, reckons as I do."

"When you report to Mr. Collier tell him you are to be sent to the home farm," Ross said decisively, eager to reward the other man. "They have need of a man to assist the smithy, and you look as if you'd do well. Provided you've a taste for country life, that is?" he added hopefully.

Beefy shoulders lifted and fell in an indifferent shrug. "Anything's better'n Lunnon, sir. Thank you." He saluted Ross once more, and bobbed a rather elegant bow in Adalaide's direction, before bounding down the steps with enough enthusiasm to set the whole structure shaking.

Adalaide watched him for a few seconds and then turned back to Ross. "Who is Mr. Collier?" she demanded, squinting up at Ross. "Why was that man following me? And what are you doing up here when you ought to be down on the Speaker's Floor receiving the best wishes of your colleagues?"

Ross's lips twitched. He wanted to shake her until her teeth rattled for giving him such a fright. He wanted to hold her close and kiss her senseless because he was so relieved to see her unharmed. But since he could do neither, he reached out and gently straightened her spectacles.

"Mr. Collier is my valet," he answered calmly. "That man was following you because I pay him to. And I am up here with you, *leannan,* because I thought you were going to be crushed and I came up to rescue you."

"Oh." She shoved her spectacles back on her nose and frowned. "Well, as you can see, I am fine. Go back to your friends. I am sure they will be needing to speak with you." And then a smile, bright and glorious as the sun, broke out over her face.

"Oh, Ross, you were wonderful!" she said, her eyes shining as she gazed up at him. "Your speech had the men about me in tears! I am so proud of you."

Ross's heart swelled with emotion. "Are you, *annsachd?"* he asked softly. "You must know 'tis all due to you. Were it not for you, I could never have accomplished half of what I have."

She shook her head, gently refuting his words. "No. 'Tis you. It was always you. You are what you have always been; a man of great nobility and character. You will go far, my lord. Very far."

Ross wasn't sure he cared for her words, for they sounded to him to be words of farewell. He took a deep breath, his hand trembling as he reached out to touch the bright red silk of her hair. "Adalaide, I—"

"Miss Terrington! Lord St. Jerome!"

Lord Hixworth came bounding toward them, followed by Falconer and the Duke of Creshton.

"Are you all right, Miss Terrington?" Hixworth took Adalaide's hand and was gazing down at her worriedly. "When Lord Falconer told me you'd been caught in the crush, I almost swooned from fear! I would never have brought you here had I known you would be in any danger."

Eager to have someone to blame for the afternoon's fiasco, Ross nailed the younger man with a chilling glance. "You brought her here?" he asked, his voice low with fury.

Hixworth gave a stiff nod. "Yes, my lord, I did."

The earl's willingness to accept responsibility for the foolishness of his actions soothed some of the anger in Ross's breast, but he was still far from mollified. "If she'd been hurt, lad, I should have been most displeased with you," he said softly. "Do you take my meaning?"

Hixworth blanched. "Yes, my lord, I do,"

"Oh, for pity's sake!" Adalaide was glaring at them both. "Will you stop terrorizing his lordship? It was *my* decision to attend your speech; does this mean you shall scold and threaten me?"

Ross glanced back at her, smiling at her cross expression. "Aye, *leannan,*" he said, his spirits soaring at the thought. "But not here. As you have reminded me, I still have a duty to carry out. The vote is waiting to be called. But," he added, flashing her a meaningful look, "we will talk. Never doubt that for one moment. We *will* talk."

"So, that's it, then," Aunt Matilda said, sighing in satisfaction as she folded the morning paper and set it to one side. "Congratulations, my dear, you have done it!"

"Thank you, Aunt," Addy replied, scraping up a smile for her aunt's benefit. In truth she'd never felt less like smiling in her life, but she knew there was no way she could tell the other woman that without also telling her why.

The papers were full of the vote to recall Wellington, and the fact that it had gone down to resounding defeat. Ross's speech had been printed verbatim, and there was a great deal of praise for the "much-honored officer." It was all they could have hoped for and more, but Addy was of no mind to celebrate.

Two days had passed since Ross's speech in Parliament. Two days during which she never left the house, waiting eagerly for a caller who never came. She knew he was busy; Lord Hixworth, who *had* bothered to call, kept her apprised of Ross's activities. She knew he was spending most of his days with Lord Creshton and the others, and a glance in the morning journals explained how he was spending his nights. Ross had become the darling of London Society, and he was feted everywhere he went. Small wonder, she thought, that he should have no time for her.

"I've been thinking, and I've decided it might be just the thing if we have a party to celebrate his lordship's victory," Aunt Matilda said, tapping a thoughtful finger to her chin. "Nothing grand, mind, no more than twenty or thirty people, I should think."

Addy stirred with interest as she contemplated her aunt's suggestion. Since most of the *ton* knew of her and her aunt's association with Ross, it would doubtlessly look odd if they didn't sponsor some sort of celebration for him. And, the secret part of her whispered slyly, if they did host such a party, then the wretch would have no choice but to attend. As things now stood, it might be her only opportunity to see him.

"That is an excellent idea!" she said, her spirits lifting with excitement. "When should we have it, do you think?"

"Oh, sooner rather than later, I should say," her aunt replied with a careless wave of her hand. "I shall leave it up to you to determine what is best."

Addy hastily excused herself and hurried up to her study, eager to begin work. She spent the next two hours composing her guest list and planning the menu. Upon consideration, she decided to serve only Scottish food, in honor of Ross's homeland. She scratched a separate note to remind herself to speak with Cook about which foods to prepare. She wasn't certain what that might involve, although she had heard rumors of something called a *haggis*. But that sounded so horridly disgusting, she was fair certain it couldn't possibly exist.

Once she decided upon the menu, she decided to make the entire evening a celebration of all things Scots. Fortunately, Scottish reels and the like were much in vogue, so finding musicians who knew how to play would be no problem. A bagpipe would be a nice touch, she thought, scribbling down more notes. She'd heard one once at a recital, and thought it quite the most stirring thing she had ever heard. Its sound had been both bold and mournful, and listening to its plaintive notes had all but brought tears to her eyes.

Perhaps that was one of the reasons she loved Ross, she mused, cupping her chin in her hand and staring dreamily off into space. Like the music of his land, he was wild and untamed, full of a rich and dark beauty underscored by deep and discordant undertones. The fanciful notion, so foreign to her usual practical nature, had her chuckling. She would next take to composing odes, she thought, her lips curving in wicked delight. To his eyes, perhaps; as green as emeralds, as cold as frost. Or to his smile; mischievous as a lad's and wicked as a rake's, depending upon his mercurial moods.

She continued working on her lists and dreaming over Ross. Her love was still new and quite precious to her, and with each passing day she learned some new and fascinating aspect of that love. For example, she learned that while she loved Ross with every fiber of her being, she could still be thoroughly hipped with him. The full measure of her love wasn't in the least diluted by her annoyance, nor was it particularly affected by the knowledge her love wasn't returned. If anything, that only added to the poignancy of that love, and she clutched it protectively to her heart.

She was busy copying out the invitations when the maid came to tell her Mr. Wellford had arrived for his daily lesson.

"Oh, dear, I forgot he was coming!" she exclaimed, setting down her quill and frowning. She was tempted to send her regrets, but upon reflection she decided it would not do. Being in love was no excuse to neglect her duties, she told herself, and went down to the drawing room to meet her pupil.

"No more, Creshton, do you hear me? I've done my duty to the general, and that is the end of it!" Ross stood in the center of the duke's massive study, his hands clenched in fury. He'd arrived at his grace's home a few minutes earlier in response to the duke's summons.

Thinking the older man wanted only to gloat over their triumph, he was somewhat taken aback when instead the duke presented him with a list of balls and the like he was expected to attend.

"Nonsense, lad," Creshton responded in his hearty way. "You're soldier enough to know that so long as the enemy is standing one's duty is never truly done. And what's so terrible, eh? A few balls, a house party or two; it's not like I'm asking you to storm the citadel, you know."

Ross was tempted to reply he'd already stormed a citadel, thank you very much, and that he far preferred that activity to attending any more tiresome balls. Drawing himself up, he gave the duke a cool look.

"Your grace," he began formally, "I've done what I said I would do, and would do more if 'twere truly needed. But it is not. I am done."

The duke leaned back in his chair, his expression thoughtful as he studied Ross. "Yes," he said slowly. "I can see that you are. Ah, well." He broke into a wide grin. "As I told Falconer, it was worth a try."

Ross hesitated, not certain what to make of the other man's response. "Then you do not mind?" he asked cautiously.

"Oh, to be sure, my lord, to be sure," the older man said with a shrug, "but there is not a great deal I can do about it, is there? If you don't wish to go, then that is the end of it."

Ross shifted on his feet, studying the duke through narrowed eyes. He suspected he was being cleverly manipulated, and he liked it not at all. The duke met his assessing stare with guileless innocence, and Ross gave a reluctant smile.

"The devil take you for a conniver, your grace," he said, shaking his head. "One more ball, and then I am truly done."

"Good of you, lad, good of you." The duke beamed at him, offering him an invitation. "The Duke of York will be expecting you tomorrow evening. Oh, and wear your uniform, won't you? Old Billy is dashed fond of uniforms."

Ross accepted the invitation in silence, damning himself for a fool. Had he known the invitation was from the prince's foulmouthed and mulish brother, he would have clung to his original refusal with a great deal more determination. However, having given his word, he was well and truly trapped. There was no going back on it now.

Never one to brood over that which could not be changed, Ross set aside his anger and sat down to sip port with the duke. The older man was regaling him with some new mischief his beloved daughter, Elinore, had fallen into when the Marquess of Falconer came striding into the room.

"Falconer, old fellow, do be seated," the duke greeted him with a gregarious wave of his sherry glass. "I was just telling St. Jerome here how Elinore near came to blows with my neighbor over his treatment of his horse!"

"The neighbor fled in terror, I assume," Falconer observed, and then turned to Ross, his remote eyes alive with fury.

"My apologies to you, my lord," he said, bowing in

Ross's direction. "It seems I gave you a poor piece of advice, and it has come back to haunt us all. You should have run that devil through when you had the chance."

Ross could think only one devil in sad want of running through, and set his glass down with exaggerated care. "What has my cousin done now?" he asked, rising slowly to his feet.

"I have no real proof it was he," Falconer warned, "and the rumors have only just reached my ears. But I knew you would want to know the moment I caught wind of it."

"What is the *burdeach* saying of me now?" Ross asked wearily, thinking he should kill his cousin for no reason other than he was proving so tedious.

"It's not you he is gossiping about this time." The grimness in Falconer's voice alerted Ross. "He has found a new target to wound with his poisonous tongue."

"Who?" Ross asked, although he already guessed the answer.

"It is Miss Terrington. The talk in the clubs is that she is your mistress."

Ross heard Creshton's gasp of outrage, but he ignored it. In his mind his hands were already about Atherton's neck, tightening slowly as he choked the breath out of the bastard. This time he would not be stopped, he vowed. Atherton was a dead man.

"Where is he?" His voice was cold, almost indifferent, as he turned to Falconer.

"No one knows," Falconer said, his lips thinning. "I know he was staying at an inn off Wigmore Street, but he has disappeared without a trace. I am sorry."

He would speak with Nevil, Ross decided with that

same icy calm. He'd had the man under close observation for the past several weeks, and if anyone knew where he was to be found, it would be the corporal.

"Your forgiveness, your grace," Falconer said to the duke, "but I need to be private with St. Jerome."

"Of course, of course," the duke said, nodding. "Let me know if there is anything I can do to be of assistance."

Ross collected his hat and gloves from the butler and hurried outside where Falconer's carriage was waiting.

"There is no need for you to accompany me, sir," Ross told the marquess coolly. "I know what needs to be done, and I am more than willing to do it. Good day to you."

Falconer eyed him coolly. "If you are referring to killing your cousin, I assure you that can wait. You've more pressing matters to attend to at the moment."

Ross shot him a startled look. "What can be more important than murdering that disgusting piece of *cacc?*"

"Salvaging Miss Terrington's reputation. Surely you didn't think breaking Atherton's neck is the only remedy that is needed?" he added as Ross continued gaping at him. "Miss Terrington's good name has been sullied, and no amount of killing will change that fact. If you wish to save her, then you must marry her as soon as it can be arranged. There is no other way."

The calm words struck Ross like the blade of a claymore. He'd decided days ago to make Addy his bride, and so it was no great matter for him to make the offer. What did matter, and what ate at his soul like acid, was the fact that she no longer had the option of refusing. It was then that the truth exploded in Ross's heart.

"My God," he said, so thunderstruck he didn't bother to censor his words. "I love her."

Rather than being shocked, or worse still, amused, Falconer merely gave a brief nod. "Yes, I rather thought that you might. Now, sir, how do you mean to get her to accept you?"

In answer Ross climbed into the carriage, and after giving the coachman Adalaide's address, Falconer climbed in after him. The journey was blessedly brief, and the wheels of the carriage had scarce stopped turning before Ross leapt out of the carriage and raced up the steps to the house. The butler barely had time to open the door before Ross was pushing his way inside.

"Adalaide?" he demanded of the startled major-domo. "Where is she?"

"M-Miss Terrington is in the drawing room, my lord," Williams stammered, wide-eyed at Ross's fierce expression. "I-I can announce you, sir, if you would like."

"I can announce myself, I thank you," Ross said, and strode down the hall to the small room where he had spent so many happy and frustrating hours. Without knocking he pushed the door open with considerable force, and stalked over to where Adalaide was standing. She'd leapt to her feet at his entrance, and was staring at him in astonishment.

"My lord, what are you doing here?" she demanded, laying a hand over her heart as if to calm its pounding.

Ross stared at her, trying to think of how to soften his words. He took a deep breath and then said, "We are getting married."

She blinked at him owlishly. "I beg your pardon."

He scowled. "Did you no' hear me? I said we're getting married. Fetch your cloak and bonnet that we may leave."

Instead of running into his arms with a delighted cry

as he wished, or shrieking down the house in rage as he'd expected, she turned to the stunned young man standing uncertainly at her side.

"That, Mr. Wellford, is quite the wrong way to make an offer in form," she told him coolly. "You are not to offer for Miss Jenkins in this manner unless you wish her to refuse.

"I-I-I s-s-see, M-M-Miss T-T-Terrington," the terrified young man stuttered, staring at Ross as if he were a demon sprung straight from hell. "I c-c-certainly s-s-shan't do t-t-that."

Satisfied, she glanced back at Ross. "Now, sir," she said to him with cool condescension, "if there will be nothing else, I am afraid I must ask you to leave."

Ross tossed his hat and gloves aside, advancing on Adalaide with the determined gait of a predator. He stopped a few inches from her, and then flicked a cold look at the younger man.

"What was your name, again?"

"W-W-W-Wellford, my l-l-lord. R-Richard Wellford."

"Mr. Wellford." Ross sent the lad a smile that nearly set him to swooning. "You may be the first to wish Adalaide and myself happy, for we are to be married within the week." And without giving Adalaide time to protest, he swept her into his arms, taking her lips in a kiss that was as singularly wondrous as it was completely scandalous.

Twelve

Ross's mouth was warm and demanding, taking her lips in a kiss that sent Addy's head spinning. It was every bit as wild and wonderful as the last kiss they had shared, and once her shock subsided, Addy was helpless to resist its power. Her arms lifted, twining about his neck as she held him close. She thought he would deepen the kiss, but he was already lifting his head, a look of cold determination shimmering in his eyes as he gazed down at her. It was that look that brought her to her senses with a jolt, and she began struggling to free herself.

"Let me go at once!" she exclaimed, pushing against Ross's chest and flushing with indignation. "What the devil do you think you are doing?"

"Claiming you," Ross said, bending his head to press a quick kiss against her lips. "Now do as I say, *mo céile,* and go fetch your bonnet. We've much we must do."

"I most certainly will not!" Addy succeeded in fighting her way free of his embrace and glared up at him in fury. "Who do you think you are to come in here and order me about like this?"

"I . . . p-p-erh-h-haps I sh-should go." Mr. Wellford began inching cautiously toward the door.

"No!" Addy whirled and stabbed her finger at him. She had no idea what Ross was about, but she was hanged if she would allow him to get away with it. "You will stay right where you are, sir!" she told Mr. Wellford. *"He* will leave!" She shot Ross a murderous glare.

"No," Ross replied calmly, "he will not." Before Addy could respond, he turned to Mr. Wellford. "I thank you, sir, for your understanding," he said with a cool smile. "Be so good as to shut the door on your way out."

Much to Addy's disgust, Mr. Wellford turned and fled the room, making such haste he was all but falling over his feet. When the door slammed behind him, Ross turned back to Addy.

"Annsachd," he began, his expression somber as he confronted her, "this is not the way I thought to ask you, but we neither of us have a choice. My cousin named you as my mistress, and so it must be marriage between us."

"Do not think to argue me out of this," he added when she began sputtering furiously. "I'll not be badgered from doing what I must do."

"What *you* must do? What of me? Am I to have no say in any of this?" she cried, feeling as if her heart was breaking. She had dreamed Ross might one day love her enough to offer marriage, but she'd never dreamed he could offer it like this, so coldly, so unemotionally, and for no reason other than because he had no other choice.

"No." His voice was resolute as he took her hand. "This is your name we are speaking of; your honor. Do you truly expect me to stand by and do nothing when both are questioned?"

The door flew open without warning and Aunt Matilda stood in the doorway, her hands on her hips as she surveyed them both. "What the devil is going on here?" she demanded querulously. "I could hear the shouting clear up in my room!" She fixed Ross with her sternest look.

"Well, sir?" she snapped suspiciously. "I trust you have an explanation for this?"

"Aye," he said, "I do." And in the starkest terms imaginable, he told Aunt Matilda what he had just told Addy. When he was done, the older woman lowered herself onto the nearest chair, visibly shaken.

"I see," she said, looking so wan, Addy went at once to her side. "Well then, my dear." She reached out to take Addy's hand, her fingers trembling and cold. "Pray accept my felicitations. We shall have the ceremony here, of course. It won't put an end to all the tattle, but it should help stop most of it."

Addy was horrified at her aunt's words. "But Aunt," she began, her voice trembling with the force of her emotions, "you don't understand. I have no desire to marry his lordship!"

Ross's response was to grow even colder. "Your pardon, Lady Fareham, but I would like to be alone with Adalaide. We have much to settle between us."

"We have nothing to settle between us!" Addy leapt to her feet, her eyes flashing in defiance. "I won't marry anyone to satisfy convention!"

Aunt Matilda silenced her with a single look. "I will speak with my niece, sir," she said, and then turned to

Ross. "You, my lord, would be better served obtaining a Special License as quickly as it can be arranged. And take Lord Falconer with you while you're about it. You cannot leave him pacing in my entry hall; he is upsetting the staff."

"Lady Fareham—"

"Now, your lordship," she interrupted, giving Ross an imperious stare. "If you please."

Ross looked as if he much desired to protest her aunt's edict, but in the end he did as he was ordered; slamming out of the room and muttering heatedly in Gaelic.

Addy wasted little time before pleading her case before her aunt. "Ma'am, you must see why this cannot be!" she implored, her eyes wet with tears as panic clawed at her. "I cannot be forced to wed against my will!"

Instead of softening, her aunt grew even more rigid. "To be sure, you cannot," she said, rising stiffly to her feet. "But that is not the issue. As for now, I should prefer speaking with you in my sitting room."

"But Aunt—"

"Your will humor me in this, Adalaide," her aunt interrupted, trembling visibly with emotion. "For I vow, I have had all I care to endure."

Much cowed, Addy trailed after her aunt. She'd never seen the older lady so stricken, and she worried if this latest scandal might prove too much for her health.

"There," Aunt Matilda said, after settling on her settee in the privacy of her room. "I trust we should be safe from the prying eyes and ears of every servant. Heaven knows you've already given them enough to gabble about."

"You speak as if this was all *my* doing," Addy complained, settling her skirts about her as she sat beside her aunt.

"Since you were the one doing all the shrieking, I should think the answer to that rather obvious," her aunt responded with a sniff. "But enough of that. Tell me the real reason why you are refusing to marry his lordship."

"And don't waste my time prattling about your pride and your independence either," she added, meeting Addy's gaze with surprising compassion. "Tell me the truth. You love him, child. Don't you?"

The tears Addy had been fighting pooled in her eyes and began trickling down her cheeks. "Yes," she said, her voice shaking at the enormity of her confession. "Yes, I love him."

Her aunt gave a satisfied nod. "I thought as much," she said, sounding smug. "Else you shouldn't have been so vehement in your determination not to marry him for propriety's sake. Any sensible female would feel the same, but I fear it makes no difference in the end. You must marry St. Jerome, and that is all there is to be said."

"But it is so unfair!" Addy said, wiping angrily at her cheeks. "We've done nothing wrong!"

"Of course you have not." Her aunt patted her hand. "But you have been in Society long enough to know how little that matters. Perception is all, and in the eyes of the world you have been compromised. You're not a green gel who goes in ignorance of such things, child. You know what this will mean not just to yourself and your entire family, but to St. Jerome as well. He has only just proven himself a hero. Would you now have him thought a villain?"

The quiet words had Addy bowing her head as she accepted the inevitable. "But it is so unfair," she whispered, her eyes closing in anguish. "Why should Ross be forced to pay the price for his cousin's villainy?"

Lady Fareham reached out a gnarled hand to gently stroke Addy's hair. "I am an old woman, my dear, and it has been my observation it is always the innocent who suffer most from the acts of the wicked."

"However, I shouldn't weep overly much on St. Jerome's account," she added with a soft chuckle. "I've a feeling he won't find marriage to you quite so onerous as you fear."

Addy froze at that, hope flickering cautiously to life in her heart. She raised her head, the tears drying on her face as she met her aunt's knowing gaze.

"Do-do you think he loves me?" she whispered, hardly daring to speak the words aloud.

In answer, her aunt gestured at a nearby table where a bouquet of beautiful creamy white roses were arranged in a cobalt blue vase. "Do you see those roses, my dear?"

Addy turned to give the bouquet a confused frown. "Yes, of course I do, but—"

"Where do you think they came from?"

Addy blinked at the question. "From the florist, I would suppose," she said, wondering if her aunt was feeling quite the thing. "Really, Aunt, what has that to do with anything?"

"I grew those roses," her aunt replied, leaning back with a sigh. "From a small cutting I took from my mother's house. I've spent years growing it; nurturing it through killing frosts and blistering sun. I can't tell you how many times I've felt like washing my hands of it and letting it die, but I never did. It's my only memento of my mother, you see, and each year when it blooms it is like having her back with me again." Her gaze met Addy's.

"Love is like that, Adalaide. It takes a great deal of care and attention, and one must be constantly vigilant to nurture it against every adversity. But when it blooms"—her smile grew dreamy—"oh, my dear, when it blooms you will know that love is worth any pain." She laid her hand on Addy's cheek.

"You truly love Ross?"

Addy nodded, too moved to speak.

"And is his love not worth fighting for?"

Addy didn't have to think before responding. "Yes, Aunt," she said, her voice fierce. "It most certainly is."

"Then fight for it," her aunt advised, leaning down to kiss Addy's cheek. "This may not be the most auspicious way to begin a marriage, but it *is* a beginning. What you and Ross make of it will be up to you."

Addy considered that for several seconds, and then a slow smile spread across her lips. On impulse, she stood up and gave the older woman a fierce hug. "I love you, Aunt Matilda," she said, hugging the irascible woman who had been both parent and dearest friend over the last seven years.

"And I love you, poppet," her aunt replied, returning Addy's embrace. They clung to each other for several seconds, and then her aunt was drawing back, her voice suspiciously gruff as she said, "Look at us, sitting around and sniveling like a pair of old women." She laughed and dabbed at her streaming eyes. "I've a wedding to plan, and you, young lady, need to make yourself presentable. You'll want to look your best when your fiancé comes to call. Off with you now."

Addy allowed herself to be dismissed, drifting toward her rooms with a dazed smile. *Fiancé,* she thought, her heart welling with happiness. She rather liked the sound of that.

Mr. Reginald Terrington announces the coming marriage of his sister, Miss Adalaide Terrington, to Rosslyn Arthur Gordon MacCailan, Viscount St. Jerome. The ceremony will be performed in the home of Lady Fareham, the bride's aunt.

The discreet notice was printed two days later in the morning addition of *The Times.* Studying it, Ross felt a disturbing mixture of relief and trepidation. Adalaide was his fiancée, but she felt as much a stranger to him as when he'd opened his eyes to find her sitting beside his bed. Now she was a soft-spoken, well-behaved stranger who possessed the spirit of a bowl of day-old porridge, he realized, lowering the paper to his desk. Where had his fiery Adalaide gone, and what was he to make of the circumspect creature who had taken her place?

When he'd returned from procuring the Special License, he'd been prepared to go to war if that was what it took to get Adalaide to marry him. Oddly enough, he'd actually been looking forward to it, the warrior in him eager to do battle. But instead of greeting him with flying crockery and heated words of defiance, Adalaide had met him with soft words and a shy smile, quietly agreeing to marry him whenever he could arrange it. He'd been so shocked, the words of love he'd meant to offer had stuck in his throat, and there they'd remained.

"No luck with any of your cousin's friends, Captain. They claim not to have any idea where he might have run to ground." Nevil's voice brought Ross back to the present, and he turned his attention back to the corporal.

"Like as not they're lying to protect him," Ross said, rising from behind his desk to begin restlessly prowling the room. He was too used to physical activity to enjoy sitting about. He thought better on his feet, and Nevil's words reminded him he had something to think of. Finding his damned cousin. Finding and killing him, Ross amended, his hard lips thinning in a smile.

Nevil shook his head. "Not likely, Captain; Atherton owes most of them money. They'd hand him to you on a platter did they know where he's got. I'm thinking he's looking to flee the country, and I want your permission to hire on some more men. We'll need to cover the docks."

"Hire them," Ross said, thinking it would be just like his cowardly cousin to run from the consequences of his actions. He wondered where the idiot thought he would go, or what he would do when he got there. Then he decided the *burraidh* probably hadn't given the matter a single thought. Men like that seldom thought beyond the moment, and beyond their own childish needs. A man like that . . . he mused, his brows pleating in thought. Where would a man like that feel the safest?

"I beg pardon, my lord." James, the diffident young

soldier who served as his secretary, hovered uncertainly in the doorway.

"Yes, James? What is it?"

"Your fiancée and her aunt are here to inspect the house. Shall I have Cook prepare the tea you ordered?"

Ross's eyebrows raised at this. "I ordered?" he repeated, knowing quite well he'd issued no such order. To his shame, it hadn't occurred to him.

It was Nevil who responded. "Ladies like their tea," he said, giving Ross an apologetic grin. "And I knew you'd have seen to it yourself once you'd thought of it."

"Thank you, Nevil," Ross said, once more thanking the Providence that had brought them together. "You are a godsend."

"You're welcome, Captain." Nevil inclined his head graciously. "Glad to be of service."

Smiling, Ross turned to James. "Please tell Miss Terrington and Lady Fareham I'll be with them directly. Oh, and have the housekeeper ready in case Miss Terrington should desire to speak with her."

After James left, Ross turned back to Nevil. "Are you still keeping Miss Terrington under observation?" he asked, donning the jacket he'd discarded upon entering the study. "The notice of our engagement will be in all of today's papers, and I want to be prepared in case my cousin decides to make fresh mischief."

"You don't think he'd hurt your lady?" Nevil asked worriedly.

"I have no proof he would," Ross replied as he opened the door. "But I want her guarded nonetheless."

"I'll see to it," Nevil promised, rising to his feet as well. "Is there anything else I can do for you, Captain?"

Ross hesitated, his hand on the door. "Actually, there is one thing," he said, glancing back at him. "My wedding is to take place four days from today, and it would honor me greatly if you would attend."

Nevil made a strangled sound, and then straightened his shoulders proudly. "It would be my honor, sir."

"Good." Ross smiled. "Just one more thing, then."

"Sir?"

Ross's smile widened. "For the love of heaven, call me Ross." And with that he went down the hall to welcome Adalaide to her new home.

"Tell me, *annsachd,* what do you think of your home?" Ross asked, accepting the cup of tea Adalaide handed him. "You're free to change anything if 'tis not to your liking."

"It's lovely, sir." The smile she offered was as brittle as spun glass. "I am sure I shall be quite happy here."

The stilted reply was not at all to his liking. He gritted his teeth and tried again. "I know 'tis small," he began in dogged determination, "but I've other homes as well. The country seat is in the Lowlands, near to Edinburgh, and is a grand place from all accounts. I was there as a young lad, but I've few memories of the place. I thought we might go there on our bridal trip, if you've a mind?"

The words had scarce left his lips before she had set aside her teacup, regarding him with the first flash of true emotion he'd seen in days. "To Scotland?" she asked, her eyes dancing with the bright blue fire he'd so missed.

"As to that, 'tis hard to say," he drawled, pulling his

ear and doing his best to hide his pleased grin. "To a *Sassenach* like yourself, aye, 'tis Scotland, but to a Highlander . . . well, 'tis not so clear a matter."

"But we may go there?" she pleaded, her cheeks blooming with a lovely color. "I should love to see your home above all things!"

Nothing she said could have pleased him more. Glad now that Lady Fareham had discreetly returned to her own home to give them privacy, he moved from his chair to join her on the settee. Taking the hand that held the sapphire ring he'd chosen for her, he twined his fingers with hers.

"My home is in the Highlands, near the village of Avienmore," he said, brushing his thumb over the brilliant blue stone. "My mother's cousin lives there now, but there's an inn in the village where we can stay if you don't mind."

"That would be fine," she said, the matter of the inn dismissed with a wave of her other hand. "In the meanwhile, tell me more about Scotland. I have always longed to go there."

Cradling her hand in his, he leaned back against the striped cushions of the settee. " 'Tis as wild and beautiful a place as you can imagine," he said, letting himself remember things he'd long shut out of his memory. "The air's so cold sometimes, it all but snaps your nose off, but 'tis so sweet you want to drink of it like the finest wines."

"You love it, don't you?" she asked, scooting closer to him, her gaze thoughtful as she studied his face.

"Aye." He returned her perusal. "I love it." *I love you,* he longed to add, but caution kept him mute. He'd only just succeeded in luring his own Adalaide out from wherever she'd been hiding, and he feared saying anything that might send her scurrying back again. Patience, he scolded himself. His love wouldn't become any less for the waiting. On their wedding night, he decided, his pulse quickening at the thought of having Adalaide in his bed. He would tell her on their wedding night.

"Ross?" Adalaide said his name cautiously, her expression anxious as she peered at him through the lenses of her spectacles. "Is everything all right? You've the queerest expression on your face."

He immediately schooled his face to show none of the passion and wild desire consuming him. "Everything's fine, *mo céile,*" he assured her, carrying their joined hands to his lips for a brief kiss. "I was but thinking of the Highlands, and how fine you'll look walking amongst the flowers, your fiery hair flaming all about you."

To his amusement, she flushed in pretty delight. "I've always hated this color," she said, in the tones of one confessing the gravest of sins. "It seems so frivolous." She reached up with her free hand to touch an errant curl.

"No." He stayed her hand with his. "I adore your hair. I have since the first moment I saw it peeking out from beneath that ridiculous cap you were wearing. You're not to wear such a thing after we are wed, is that understood? I'll not have it."

An elegant auburn eyebrow arched in haughty amusement. *"You'll* not have it?" she said, the fierce, argumentative nature he had come to love obvious in her tone.

"And pray, sir, how do you mean to stop me if I choose to wear a hundred caps?"

" 'Tis easy, *annsachd*," he drawled, burying his fingers in her hair and tugging her closer. "Wear a hundred caps, and a hundred times I'll remove them. Along with anything else I may find not to my liking," he added, and unable to resist, covered her mouth with his own.

The kiss was as wild and sweet as his Highlands, and even as he lost himself to its magic, Ross was holding himself sternly in check. A few more days, he thought, gently teasing her tongue with his own. A few more days, and there would be no reason to stop.

It was the eve of her wedding, and Addy didn't know if she should weep or rage. Gifts had been pouring into the house since the day the notice had appeared in the paper. Gifts and invitations, she thought, grimacing at the pile stacked on her desk. She'd hoped Aunt Matilda would help her, but her aunt had insisted it was the bride's responsibility to accept or refuse the invitations sent to her as a soon-to-be-wedded woman.

Refuse most like, she decided, scowling in distaste at the thought of attending endless balls and routs. Even with Ross at her side, participating in the social round would be a torture beyond enduring, and she wondered how many she dared turn down before incurring Society's wrath. Not many, that much she knew. She and Ross had scraped through this latest scandal, but it had been a near thing. If she turned down more than a handful, it would look as if she was ashamed, and that, she knew, would be all it would take to set tongues viciously wagging.

Sighing in disgust, she picked up another letter, frowning at the almost illegible scrawl. *What on earth?* she wondered, carefully unfolding the paper.

Miss Terrington,
Bring fifteen thousand pounds to Number Twelve Ratcliffe Highway, or I shall tell the world your precious husband is a base-born bastard with no claim to the St. Jerome title.
Come alone, or you shall have cause to regret it.
A friend

"Oh, for pity's sake!" Addy exclaimed, her eyes flashing in annoyance. "This is getting tiresome!"

She tapped the letter against her hand, thinking quickly. She knew enough of her fiancé to imagine the howl he would set up if he learned of his cousin's poor attempt at blackmail. Which meant, she decided, that she simply wouldn't tell him . . . at least, not right away. She would deal with the matter on her own, and then when they were safely away in Scotland, she would mention it in passing.

She considered the matter for several seconds before reaching her conclusion. Pausing only long enough to scribble off a note, she ran up to her room to gather up her belongings. Her maid was there before her, packing for the bridal trip, and when she saw what Addy retrieved from the top of the wardrobe, her eyes went wide in alarm.

"Why, Miss Terrington, whatever would you be needing *that* for?" She indicated the small pistol with a shaking finger.

"I'm going hunting for rats," Addy replied, dropping the pistol into her reticule and pulling the strings closed. She quickly donned her oldest cloak and plainest bonnet before hurrying back down to the study. Retrieving the note and a handful of bank notes from the top of her desk drawer, she went back out into the hall to where Williams was standing at his usual post.

"I need to go out, Williams," she said, pulling on her gloves in brisk, determined movements. "Pray fetch a hack for me."

"I beg your pardon, Miss Terrington," Williams said, his Adam's apple bobbing up and down. "But Lord St. Jerome has left explicit instructions that whenever you had need of a carriage, we were to send for his. He also said you were not to be allowed out without proper escort."

The temper Addy had kept firmly under control for the past several days stirred to life. "Indeed?" she said, her lips thinning in displeasure. "And his lordship is now master here?"

"Indeed not, miss," Williams assured her quickly. "But he did say—"

"Then since he is not master here, you don't need to worry whether or not his wishes are obeyed, do you?" she asked coolly. Before he could answer, she decided to take pity on him, handing him the note she'd just written.

"Please have this delivered to his lordship at once," she said, softening the command with a smile. "It will explain everything."

Williams accepted the letter with visible reluctance.

"As you wish, Miss Terrington. But are you quite sure you won't take a footman or even a maid with you?"

Addy thought of the oblique threat in the note and shook her head. She didn't fear Atherton in the least, but the fewer witnesses to the coming confrontation, the better.

"That won't be necessary, Williams. I shan't be gone that long," she told him, some of her old confidence returning. "Be sure Lord St. Jerome gets that note. Now kindly fetch me a carriage. The sooner I am gone, the sooner I shall return."

"Ratcliffe Highway?" Ross shook his head. "Can't say as I've ever heard of it."

"No reason why you should have," Falconer said, shrugging. "Not unless you've a taste for the docks. Your cousin's pockets must be more to let than we thought, if that's where he's gone to ground. Guard your back, St. Jerome. Desperate men are dangerous men. God knows what he may do."

"It matters not to me. It's what *I* am to do that concerns me most," Ross replied coldly, his attention turned to Atherton. Since the moment the marquess had appeared with news his missing cousin had been located, his only thought was how best to take his revenge against the man who had dared slander Adalaide. As badly as he wanted to kill him, he accepted the *deamhan* wasn't worth swinging for. That didn't mean he intended letting the tattling devil escape unscathed. One way or another he would avenge his lady's honor.

"I had a word with your aide-de-camp," Falconer continued. "He has men in place watching your cousin's every move. He said Atherton sent a message earlier, and we're trying to find out to whom it was sent, and if possible, what it said. He may be trying to contact some friend we don't know about."

Ross gave a mirthless smile. "Atherton has no friends I don't know of. They've all been here, their hats in one hand and his vowels in another, hoping I'll see fit to settle his debts. I've let them know that if they want to see a farthing of what he owes them, they'll let me know the moment he contacts them."

"Then perhaps it doesn't matter," Falconer said, stroking a thoughtful finger across his lower lip. "What say you, my lord? Do we wait for further intelligence, or do we move?"

Ross needed no other prompting. He rolled to his feet, his face set in hard and deadly lines. "We move."

They were waiting for the carriage to be brought around when his butler appeared, a note on a silver tray.

"From Miss Terrington, my lord," he said, offering it to Ross. "The footman who brought it asked that it be given to you right away."

Ross accepted it curiously. It was the first note he could remember Adalaide sending him since their engagement had been announced, and he wondered what it contained. He started opening it, and then paused. Until this matter with his cousin was resolved he could not afford to be distracted. Whatever Adalaide had to say, it would have to wait. He tucked the note in his pocket.

A short while later the carriage came to a halt in front of a half-timbered building bearing the unlikely name The Golden Pear. Ross stared at it in silence, torn with an odd mixture of emotions. Six months ago the place would have seemed a palace to him; now it looked like nothing more than a hovel. He brushed the thought aside and climbed out.

"We should have brought a brace of cannons with us," Falconer observed, staring up at the building in wry amusement. "We'll be lucky to escape here without getting our throats slit and our pockets picked clean."

A wolfish smile touched Ross's lips. "Let them try," he said, drawing a pistol from beneath his greatcoat. "In the meanwhile, let's go find my cousin. I would have words with him."

The sight of armed men entering the inn didn't warrant so much as a glance from the other occupants of the public room. They merely went on with their drinking and gaming, paying Ross and Falconer not the slightest mind as they went up to the innkeeper.

"You've a swell staying here," Falconer said, sliding a coin across the bar. "Where is he?"

The coin disappeared in the innkeeper's filthy hand. " 'E's busy, don't yer know?" the man advised them, giving them a leering wink. "Come back when 'e an' the doxy what's in there with 'im be finished. Shouldn't be longer 'n 'alf an 'hour. She 'tweren't no fancy piece for all 'er airs."

Ross had started to say something when he felt a cold trickle of unease down his spine. The small warning had saved his life too many times for him to discount it now. "What did this lady look like?" he asked, a cold feeling of dread settling in the pit of his stomach. "What color was her hair?"

" 'Ard to say, guv," the innkeeper said with another

wink. "She were wearin' one o' them capes an' a bonnet, 'idin' most of 'er. But fer a bit more gold I could be more surelike."

Ross didn't waste any time in arguing. He simply pulled the man across the counter and placed the barrel of the pistol beneath the man's stubble-covered chin. "Be sure," he advised, cocking the pistol. "Be very sure."

"Red!" the innkeeper cried out, his eyes bulging with fear. "It were red, an' she were wearin' spectacles. Thought she looked more like a governess than a mort, but the gents what come here ain't regular in what they fancy."

Ross tried not to think what had brought Adalaide there. He wanted only to rescue her. Then he wanted to ring a peal over her head she'd not soon be forgetting. He gave the innkeeper another shake. "Where are they?"

"Room at the back." The innkeeper's words fell over each other in his eagerness to speak them. "I call it a parlor for them what wants a bit o' privacy an' is willin' to pay fer it. She ain't been there but a quarter hour, if that. If you waits 'til she's done, I—" His words ended in a gurgle when Ross gave him an angry shake before flinging him backward.

Disgusted, Ross reached into his pocket, flinging down another coin before turning back to Falconer.

"If he's so much as touched her, he is dead," he said, his voice flat. "Understand that."

"I understand," Falconer promised. "Let's go." They turned toward the back, but before they'd taken a step the sound of a single gunshot rang out.

Ross didn't remember moving. One moment he was standing beside Falconer, and the next he was inside the tiny room, his pistol in one hand and his eyes full of agony. A low groan reached his ears and he glanced down, his eyes widening in stunned disbelief at the sight of his cousin lying on the floor, cradling his arm.

"She shot me," Atherton moaned, rolling from side to side. "The bitch shot me."

"Of course I shot you, you odious creature," Adalaide said crossly, her elfin features set in a disapproving scowl. "I told you I would. Now, are you going to get on that ship, or must I put another bullet in you?" She blinked as Falconer came charging into the room.

"Oh, there you are, Ross," she greeted him with a smile. "You got my note, I gather?"

"Yes, *annsachd*," he said, his voice sounding oddly calm, even to his own ears, "I got your note."

"Excellent." She beamed at him, as she used to do when he'd gotten a lesson right. "Then you must know I have the right of it and this wretched creature cannot be allowed to continue practicing his villainy. If he cannot be persuaded to emigrate, then we shall simply have to kill him. I refuse to let him remain a threat to our children."

Atherton set up a howl at this, but Ross didn't pay him any mind. He stared at Adalaide, the pistol in her hand, her spectacles slightly askew, and her face set with determination.

"No, *annsachd*," he agreed, fighting to keep his joy from showing. "We cannot allow that."

"Someone call the Watch!" Atherton wailed, rising unsteadily to his feet. "That woman is mad! She ought to be locked up for the public good! She came in here and shot me without the slightest provocation!"

"I've had plenty of provocation, you sniveling coward!" Adalaide jabbed the pistol in his direction. "I will not have you spreading lies about the man I love. If I cannot have your silence one way, then I shall have it another. Ross might be too much of a gentleman to shoot you down as you deserve, but I am not possessed of such tiresome scruples." And she calmly began reloading her weapon.

"I'll go! I'll go, curse you!" Atherton wailed, backing away from her. "The devil take you both! You deserve one another!"

"Aye," Ross said, unable to hold back a roar of laugher, "and so we do." He reached out and plucked Adalaide's pistol from her hand, ignoring her indignant protests as he handed the pistol and powder bottle to Falconer. He next turned to Atherton.

"Listen well, cousin, for this is the last time we shall speak," he said, feeling a sharp pang of regret he'd been denied his chance to so much as break the *cladhaire's* nose. "Stay away from me and mine. If you return to England or Scotland ever again, I'll give her back her pistol. Is that understood?"

"Perfectly." Atherton's voice was sulky, but it contained just enough fear to satisfy Ross. He glanced up at Falconer, who was also looking as if he longed to break out laughing.

"See my cousin gets some doctoring before you put him on a ship, if you would, my lord," Ross said, knowing he could trust the other man to see to the matter for him. "I hear the south of the Pacific is in want of villains. Send him there."

"As you wish," Falconer said, bowing formally to

Ross. "My lord." He turned next to Adalaide. "My lady." And he led the protesting Atherton away, closing the door behind them.

"Now, Ross, I know what you are going to say," Adalaide said, regarding him anxiously. "But in my own defense, I should like to say I only did as you yourself would have done. The wretch was threatening to have you named a bastard, for heaven's sake, and I knew I had to do something."

"And so you shot him," Ross said, advancing on her slowly.

"Well, not right away," she replied, clearly puzzled by his apparent calm. "I tried reasoning with him first, and when that failed to have any effect, that's when I shot him."

"It was only a flesh wound," she added hastily. "My brothers taught me to shoot, and I am really quite good."

"So it would seem." He stopped a few feet from her.

"Well, is that all you can say?" she demanded, hands on her hips as she glared at him.

"No, there is something else I should like to say." He was shaking inside from the need to hold her, but there was something he needed to say, something he wanted to say more than anything in the world.

"And what is that?" She was eyeing him with suspicion. "If you're thinking of trying to cry off, you may think again. The announcement has already been made and that is that."

"No, I've no intention of crying off."

"Then what?" She all but shouted the words, and that was when he saw the fear, the longing she had kept hidden from him. The sight of it had him moving forward, taking her into his arms and holding her to his heart with fierce joy.

"I love you, Adalaide Margurite," he said softly, brushing his lips across hers. "I love you more than my life, more than my honor. Marry me, *leannan,* and I swear to you I will do everything in my power to make you happy."

Her blue eyes sparkled with tears of happiness. "And I love you," she murmured, standing on tiptoe to boldly press her mouth to his. "Now, will you do one thing for me?"

Ross kissed her again, deeper this time, and with a great deal more warmth than was strictly proper. "What is that, my dearest?" he asked, his voice husky with passion.

She smiled beguilingly. "Teach me what those words you are always calling me really mean."

He stared down at her, his heart overflowing with a happiness and a love greater than anything he could ever have imagined. "Gladly, *mo cridhe,*" he said, and proceeded to give her a lesson in Gaelic that was nearly as shocking as it was delightful.

AUTHOR'S NOTE

The Author wishes to beg the Readers' indulgence as she has played rather fast and loose with historical facts. Whereas 'tis true there were several attempts to have Wellington removed as commander of the Expeditionary Forces on the Peninsula, none of these attempts occurred during the time frame indicated in this novel. The Author shamelessly manipulated these facts to fit the dramatic necessity of the story, and hasn't a jot of remorse for having done so.

More Zebra Regency Romances